Sweet Surrender

Jenn A.
Sesto

Sweet Surrender © 2007 by Jenn A. Sesto
All rights reserved. Published 2007

Scripture taken from the New King James Version®. Copyright © 1982
by Thomas Nelson, Inc. Used by permission. All rights reserved.

Published by
VMI Publishers
Sisters, Oregon
www.vmipublishers.com

ISBN: 1-933204-47-8
ISBN 13: 978-1-933204-47-5

Library of Congress Control Number: 2007933438

Printed in the USA.

Cover design by Joe Bailen.

Dedicated

to my loving husband, Mike and my two daughters, Morgan and Magen, for their love, patience and encouragement throughout the development of this book. And to Michele and Regina, for mentoring and inspiring me and helping me grow closer to God, experiencing His Grace and Redemption through faith.

Chapter One

ecky Lee, quick, get up!"

"Go away," Becky Lee moaned. She covered her face with her blankets. Maybe if she lay still long enough, her sister would just leave. But no.

Denise pulled up the blinds with such force, they slammed at the top of the windowsill. "Hung over, I assume. I should have known not to trust you, leaving you alone last night."

"Oh, shut up. Let me go back to sleep."

"No," Denise shrieked. She grabbed the covers and yanked them to the floor. "Mom and Dad are going to be home in less than an hour, and you and your so-called friends left the living room trashed. If I'd have known, I would have come home sooner."

"You're just afraid Mom and Dad will find out you were out all night with Derek and left me home alone."

Denise moved to the doorway, then turned back to Becky Lee. "I'm an adult. I can stay out all night with whoever I want. Mom and Dad don't care."

"Yeah, except when you're supposed to be home watching your baby sister."

"*Baby* is right. If you acted seventeen, maybe I wouldn't have to babysit you." Denise stormed out of the room, letting out a big sigh.

"Quit being such a nag," Becky Lee yelled as she sat up. An intense ache filled her head, then shot to her stomach. She leaped out of bed, ran past Denise in the hall, and barely made it to the bathroom. She dropped to her knees in front of the commode.

Denise stopped in the doorway. "If you didn't drink so much—"

Becky Lee reached behind her and slammed the door in Denise's face. If only her sister would have let her sleep it off, she'd be fine. But now she would have to deal with her hangover.

❦ ❦ ❦

After brushing her teeth and changing into shorts and a tank top, Becky Lee went downstairs. The stagnant smell of warm beer and leftover pepperoni pizza turned her stomach again. She went to the front door, opened it, and drew in a deep breath. The air was still a little chilly, as it often was on September mornings. A slight breeze made its way through the screen door and cooled her flushed face.

Finally she turned back and started cleaning up the mess. She wished she'd made her friends help clean up. But that thought never occurred to her while they were partying. There wasn't much she thought about or cared about when she was drunk. It was all about having fun or, sometimes, about numbing the pain. It was her escape from reality either way.

The good thing was that last night she'd had fun. Her boyfriend wasn't being a jerk and they had a great time together. Jesse was extra nice and loving toward her, which was something he hadn't been in the last few days. With him, it was always that way, a few days of nice, holding and loving her as if she were the most important thing in the world to him, and then a few days of distance and no talking. But she'd gotten used to the roller-coaster ride and took the good days with the bad.

Becky Lee dropped the last beer can in her bag just as Denise came in from the kitchen, carrying a full garbage bag.

She set the bag at Becky Lee's feet. "Put that in the back of my truck. I've got to get rid of the evidence."

Becky Lee's face twisted in disgust. "Don't be so self-righteous. You did the same thing when you were my age."

"And now I realize how stupid it was. Besides, now that I'm twenty-one, it's not so exciting anymore."

Becky Lee carried both bags toward the door. "Well, then, just leave me alone and let me have fun."

"Here, let me get that for you." Denise opened the screen door. For the first time since Becky Lee woke up, she smiled. "I remember what it was like, and you're right. I'll lay off the mother trip if you'll be more responsible with your partying. I just don't want to have to clean up after you every time."

The phone rang.

Becky Lee stepped onto the porch and managed a half-smile. "Get that, would ya? It might be Jesse."

The door swung shut behind Becky Lee as Denise went off to answer the call. She crossed the covered, wrap-around deck and went down the three steps to the gravel path below. She stopped for a moment, her eyes closed. The warmth of the sun washed over her face. The fresh air gave temporary relief to her headache.

She decided how she was going to get rid of her hangover. She'd lay out in the sun for as long she could before it got too hot. Then maybe she'd ride her horse to the swimming hole to cool off. She'd call Jesse and have him go with her. They didn't get much alone time last night, not with all their friends there. They could have that time this afternoon, just the two of them. It had been a while since it was just the two of them and she missed being in his arms. This would be a perfect opportunity.

Pleased with her decision, Becky Lee walked off to the side of house where Denise's truck was parked. After lifting the bags into the bed of the truck, she looked out at the one acre of pasture where their herd of cows stood grazing.

Beyond the pasture, she saw someone standing in the next driveway, waving. *Jesse.* More than likely with no hangover. It bothered her that he could drink so much more than her and then feel fine in the morning. He'd tell her that her five-foot-six, 122-pound body was no match for his six-foot-two, 210 pounds. He'd follow with "You'll never catch up with me when it comes to drinking." She'd reply that she had fun trying, though.

She waved back, then went into the house to call him. "Hey, Denise, I'm gonna—"

Denise sat on the edge of Daddy's recliner, her elbows on her thighs. Her long brown hair covered much of her hands, which were holding her face. Was she crying? She choked on a sob, then took in a deep breath. She looked up. Her face was streaked with mascara and tears.

Becky Lee's stomach tightened.

Denise dropped her arms to her knees and wrung her hands. She looked at the floor for what seemed an eternity.

Becky Lee didn't know if she should go over to Denise or give her some space. "Who was on the phone?"

She shook her head. "Mom and Dad…"

Becky Lee's breathing stopped. Numbness overwhelmed her. The walls closed in. "What happened?"

Denise started to speak, then stopped. Tears rolled down her face. "Car accident. Th-this morning. They were both…killed."

Chapter Two

Becky Lee waited in the living room, cell phone in hand. Jesse was an hour late. She leaned back in her daddy's recliner. The foot rest popped out. Even with all the cigarette burns and whiskey stains, sitting here made her feel like her daddy was right there with her. She longed to talk to him and tell him about her problems with Jesse. He'd always understood and often told her that Jesse reminded him of himself.

Becky Lee opened her phone and scrolled through the picture gallery. She found a photo of her parents. She'd taken it just before they left for their last weekend trip. Her phone was new at the time, so she was playing around taking all kinds of pictures. She was now glad she took this one. They were in a hurry to leave, but Becky Lee coerced them into posing by the car just before getting in. They looked impatient but were both smiling.

It was hard to believe they'd been gone for six months now. She still struggled with how the accident occurred. She was told that a deer had run out in front of them. They swerved to miss it, but lost control of the car, slamming head-on into a tree.

Becky Lee glanced at the small, round table next to her. It too had burns and a couple of spots where the shiny wood bubbled up from spilled whiskey sitting on it too long. An empty ashtray sat on it, beside a picture of their family. Daddy was handsome in the suit her mom had put together for him from the thrift store. He never would buy a real suit, he said, because most people wouldn't recognize him all dressed up.

And her mom ...so beautiful. Her light brown hair was curled, the sides pulled back. Her makeup accentuated her blue eyes. Becky Lee had told her often that she should wear makeup more often, but this was practically the only time she had. Mom was a simple woman and perfectly happy working on the ranch, never worried about fussing over herself. Jeans and T-shirts were practically her entire wardrobe. She'd just throw her hair up in a clip and off she went.

But Mom had a thing for getting annual pictures taken. Everyone had to dress up, like it or not. Becky Lee and Denise complained every year that it was a waste of time and money. Now, for the first time, Becky Lee realized how much she appreciated that her mom made them do it. They'd had this one done just a month prior to the accident.

A tear rolled down Becky Lee's cheek. "I miss you both."

Her phone vibrated. She brushed the tear off her face and read her best friend's text message: *He there yet?*

No, Becky Lee typed back. *R u done?*

No.

What color did u get?

Blonde.

The screen door slammed. Becky Lee looked up. Denise held a stack of mail in one hand and an open letter in the other. Her eyes narrowed as she read. Whatever it was had Denise's undivided attention. Finally, she looked up at Becky Lee, waving the letter in the air. "Do you know what this is?"

"Nope, but I'm sure you're gonna tell me." Becky Lee was in no mood to deal with one of her sister's motherly lectures.

Denise cut across the living room. Anger flashed in her eyes. Apparently, Denise wasn't in the mood for her either.

Becky Lee typed *gotta go,* then closed her phone.

"I'm sure you were aware that this deficiency notice was coming." She dropped it into Becky Lee's lap. "Or are you going to tell me you didn't realize you were failing four out of your six classes?"

"Who cares?" Ignoring the paper, Becky Lee played with the buttons on the side of her phone.

Denise picked up the paper and shook it in Becky Lee's face. "*You* should care. You're failing! Why does that not bother you?" Denise's voice sounded desperate.

"I just haven't finished my assignments yet. All I have to do is turn them in before the end of the quarter and my grades will go up."

"So you do nothing all quarter and turn everything in at the end? You get full credit for this?"

"Not in all my classes, but some. As long as I get a D, I still pass."

Denise clenched her teeth. Her jaw twitched. She looked at the paper, then back at Becky Lee. "What about you being frequently absent?"

"So I skipped a couple classes. Big deal."

"Are you cutting with Jesse?"

"Sometimes."

"You need to quit seeing him."

"You can't stop me."

Denise closed her eyes and drew in a deep breath. For a moment, she just stood there. Then she leaned in closer to Becky Lee. In a low, steady voice she said, "I'm going to call your counselor tomorrow and request a weekly progress report on your attendance and grades. Unless I see some drastic improvement, I will put a stop to your weekend partying. And I won't let you go out with Jesse anymore." She backed away.

Becky Lee jumped up. "No! If I can't go out with Jesse, he'll find—"

"Someone else? Wouldn't that be just like him?"

Becky Lee stood as tall as she could to face Denise eye-to-eye. "You just don't like him. You never did."

"You're right. I don't. I don't know why Mom and Dad let you date him in the first place."

"They were okay with it, so you can't say anything."

Denise folded the paper and placed it back inside the envelope, then looked Becky Lee in the eyes. "You have four weeks until this quarter ends. If you don't bring these grades up to at least a C, I will sell this place early."

Becky Lee choked. "But I'll only have one quarter left before graduation."

"The way you're going, you're not going to graduate anyway." Denise turned to leave.

"This is just your excuse to move to the city now and get away from this ranch. You're using me to get your way."

Denise turned back. "I agreed to let you finish school here. You've known all along that I was going to sell after you graduated. If you aren't going to put forth the effort to even make it to graduation, I'll sell now so I can get on with my life."

"What about my life? If you sell the ranch, what am I supposed to do? You know I want to keep this place."

"You couldn't handle it by yourself. There's too much to do."

"I'll hire new ranch hands. Maybe some of the ones you laid off will want to come back."

Denise held up her hand. "I've told you before, the ranch hasn't been able to pay for itself in a long time. You just don't listen to me. Get it through your head: I'm selling."

"Fine, you do that."

Denise rolled her eyes and turned to leave just as the screen door opened.

"Arguing again?" Jesse strutted into the house as if he owned the place. He flashed a cocky smile as he passed Denise.

Denise's face flushed with anger. She turned to her sister. "Remember what I said about the grades." She stormed into the kitchen.

Becky Lee watched her throw the mail onto the kitchen table. A couple of envelopes slid off onto the floor. She opened the refrigerator and pulled out a package of hamburger meat and slammed it on the counter.

Jesse grabbed Becky Lee at the waist and pulled her close to him.

"Sorry I'm late." He bent down to kiss her, but she pushed him away.

She usually melted into his arms and let him have his way with her, but right now she was too angry about everything. Him being late. The selling of the ranch. Her sister only thinking of herself. Even her grades, although she really didn't care about them much.

"Where've you been?"

"I got delayed. I said I was sorry."

Jesse tried to move back in on her, but she ducked away and went for the door. "You always get delayed." She pushed open the screen.

A black BMW, with no license plates, pulled into the driveway. Becky Lee couldn't see the driver through the tinted windows. "Who in the world is that?"

The car door opened and a petite blonde girl got out of the driver's seat. She wore a short denim skirt and a low-cut red tank top. Her long curls bounced over her shoulders as she walked up the path to the steps. She stopped when Becky Lee stepped out of the house. Her bright red lips curved. "Hi," she said, her voice like syrup. Sickening.

"Who are you?" Becky Lee bit out.

"Is Jesse here? I thought I saw him walk up this driveway."

"Are you the reason he was *delayed*?"

The girl's eyes narrowed. "What?"

"I'm here." Jesse opened the screen door and pushed past Becky Lee, almost knocking her down.

"Oh, Jesse, you are here. Good." She tossed her curls over her shoulder and smiled up at him. She put two fingers into one of the pockets on her skirt and pulled out a piece of paper. "I forgot to give you my cell-phone number. You know, in case you get lost."

Becky Lee leaped toward the steps and grabbed the piece of paper. "What does he need your phone number for?"

"I'll take that," Jesse said and snapped it out of Becky Lee's hand. "Victoria's parents are having a party Friday—"

"More like a gathering really," Victoria said. "Jesse and his family have been invited by my parents to celebrate some real-estate transactions."

Becky Lee tensed. She clenched her teeth and glared at Jesse. "What real-estate transactions? Your family has no more money than mine."

He placed his hand on Becky Lee's shoulder. "Go get the horses ready. I'll be there in a sec. Okay?"

Becky Lee sneered at Victoria. "Don't you think it's a little too cold to be wearing nothing out here?"

She knew it wasn't that cold out, but she had to have the last word, even if it was a random comment. She slammed the screen door behind her, then stomped into the kitchen. As she hurried toward the back door, she collided with her sister.

"Hey!" Denise maneuvered quickly, trying to keep the plate of raw hamburger patties from falling out of her hands. "Slow down."

"I didn't bump you that hard."

"Where's Jesse?"

"He's out front schmoozing with some girl."

"Who?"

"I don't know, but I think she's from the city."

"What makes you say that?"

"Nobody who lives out here can afford a car like that."

"Here," Denise said, holding out the plate of patties. "Wrap this with foil and put it in the fridge."

Becky Lee took the plate of hamburgers and set it on the counter.

Denise washed her hands. "So, what does this girl want with Jesse?"

"I don't know."

"Well, I imagine you'll find out soon enough."

"You bet I will."

Denise rinsed her soapy hands under the running water in the sink. "Do you think Jesse will be staying for dinner? Or maybe I should ask, will you let him stay for dinner?" There was a hint of anticipation in Denise's eyes. She was undoubtedly hoping the answer would be no.

Becky Lee shrugged. She opened a drawer by the refrigerator, pulled out the foil, and ripped off a piece. Wrapping the plate, she replied, "I don't know."

Denise dried her hands, then leaned against the counter. "Derek and I have an appointment at River's End Hall to finalize some wedding details. We'll get a bite to eat in the city. The hamburgers are for you and Jesse, if he stays. Freeze any that you don't cook, okay?"

Becky Lee set the hamburger plate in the fridge. She didn't care about Denise's plans, but she was glad to hear that she was leaving. Denise was the last person she wanted around right now. All Denise cared about was herself and her stupid fiancé.

"I'll be home by nine," Denise continued. "I expect your homework done and Jesse gone by then."

Becky Lee looked up and started to appeal, but Denise held up a hand. "If not, he won't be allowed over here anymore."

"Whatever!" Becky Lee slammed out the back door and stormed toward the horse barn.

❦ ❦ ❦

The huge double wooden door creaked as it swung open. It hit hard against the side of the twelve-stall barn. Peggy, a beautiful, sixteen-hands-high palomino, pawed at the ground in the last stall. Becky Lee smiled as she walked toward Peggy, listening to her trot from her stall out into her paddock and then back inside. Her big head appeared over the stall gate, looking down the breezeway. Peggy whinnied.

Becky Lee grabbed the halter and lead rope and opened the gate. "Hey there, Peg. You ready for a ride?"

Peggy trotted back outside, her cream-colored mane and tail flicking with each step. She tossed her head playfully and bucked in the air. Becky Lee's heart melted. Peggy was the only one who ever seemed excited to see her. She loved Peggy even more than Jesse. Peggy didn't hurt her.

"Come on now, Peg."

Peggy trotted back into the stall and lowered her head. Becky Lee strapped on the halter. "Jes is riding with us today."

Another whinny.

"Don't get too excited. I'm mad at him right now."

Becky Lee led Peggy into the breezeway and grabbed the grooming bucket, which sat between Peggy's stall and King's.

King, named for his proud personality, stood halfway in his stall and half in his paddock, his head high. He watched Becky Lee as she walked by. He was the same size as Peggy, but he was a chestnut color, with black socks, mane, and tail.

Becky Lee stopped in front of his gate. He backed out of his stall and pranced around the paddock. He stopped, looked at Becky Lee, then whinnied.

"I'll be back to get you, King," Becky Lee hollered.

"It's a good thing he's locked up," she murmured to Peggy. "If not, he'd be running all over the pasture trying to catch you." Becky Lee shook her head. "Just like Jesse, huh?"

❦ ❦ ❦

Becky Lee waited with the two horses at the tie-off post just outside the barn. She had double-checked the cinches on both saddles to make sure they were snug and properly buckled. She placed the bit in Peggy's mouth and affixed the headstall over her ears. She buckled the chin strap and lifted the reins over Peggy's head, then wrapped them around the horn on the saddle a couple of times to prevent them from falling to the ground. She did the same for King.

"So, where is he?" Becky Lee scratched the horses' foreheads. "You guys think he'll show?" They pushed their heads closer to her, begging for more attention.

Jesse walked through the side gate and up to the tie-off post, grinning like a little kid who'd just gotten his way. "Ready?" he asked, petting King.

"If you're done drooling over what's-her-face."

"I wasn't drooling. She's just a friend."

Becky Lee mounted Peggy. She gathered her reins and adjusted herself in the saddle. She shot Jesse a glare and he gave her a big, innocent smile. *He must think I'm stupid.*

"Yah!" She kicked Peggy's sides and gave her her head. Peggy broke into a run and galloped through the back pasture gate. "See you at the swimming hole," Becky Lee shouted over her shoulder as she raced toward the eighty acres of open land beyond the ranch.

The freedom that came with riding across the field on horseback was the best feeling in the world to Becky Lee. Her problems seemed to disappear in the wind.

It was a beautiful day, warmer than usual for the end of February. Just a few clouds in the sky and a slight breeze. Wild flowers of every color appeared through the tall grass. The trees along the river's edge up ahead had a few buds. Spring had come early.

Becky Lee slowed Peggy to a trot as they came close to the swimming hole. Peggy snorted, her breathing heavy. "Sorry, girl. Guess I should have let you warm up first. You thirsty?"

The mare slowed to a walk as they approached the thick brush and trees. Becky Lee ducked to avoid a branch as they went through a small opening just big enough for the horse to get through. A few steps along the makeshift path, and they were at the top of a steep embankment. Becky Lee leaned back in the saddle as the mare maneuvered down, switching back and forth until they were at the bottom.

At the shoreline, Becky Lee jumped off and let Peggy drink. The water was about thirty feet across and another thirty feet from inlet to outlet, running east to west. Off to the right, a rope swing dangled from a huge oak tree. Her dad had tied it there years ago. She and Denise used to spend their summers down here, while the horses grazed on the wild grass along the bank. She had dreams that someday her kids would come down here and have as much fun as she had.

Jenn A. Sesto

The realization of selling the ranch came rushing into her mind. If Denise sold the place, she would probably never be able to come back here again. *After she gets married, I'll have nothing.*

A rustling noise at the top of the embankment startled Peggy. "Easy, girl. I'm sure it's just King."

Becky Lee scratched Peggy's neck as she watched King and Jesse come out of the thick brush. Jesse's red face and pursed lips told her he wasn't happy.

At the shore, Jesse slid off King. "Why did you take off like that?" he asked as King lowered his head to drink.

"Peggy wanted to run, so I let her. What's the big deal?"

"I think you're mad 'cause Vicki came over."

"Oh, you're so observant," Becky Lee replied, sarcasm dripping in her voice.

Jesse's anger turned to cockiness. "You're jealous." He laughed.

Becky Lee pounded a finger into Jesse's chest. "Were you gonna tell me you had a date with a city girl, or were you planning on lying to me? Maybe tell me your poor aunt is sick or something? Look, if you don't want me anymore, just say so."

"Now, Becky Lee." Jesse reached for her.

She backed away. "Don't touch me!"

"Why do you always make something out of nothing?"

"What would you do if I made a date with you, then I told you someone in my family was sick, just so I could go out with someone else?"

"I didn't tell you anyone was sick, and we don't have a date set. Do we?"

"That's not the point!"

Jesse looked away and fell silent.

Becky Lee waited. He had to say something else. Anything that might make her feel better. But he said nothing. Anger welled up inside her. She didn't understand why he always had to dangle her out on a thread, left to wonder what he was thinking or what his next move was going to be.

Jesse moved around King and inspected the saddle. He loosened the cinch and retightened it. "If you want to go out with someone else, just tell me."

Becky Lee gaped at him. That wasn't what she wanted to hear.

Jesse mounted King again. "Vicki and I are going to a party her parents are throwing. She needed someone to go with her, and she asked me. It's purely innocent."

Becky Lee stared at the far side of the swimming hole. Her heart ached. But she had no say in this. Jesse didn't like being told he couldn't do something. If she didn't allow him to go on this "date," he'd leave her. She couldn't handle that. He was the only thing keeping her together since her parents died. She pushed her anger down. Deep.

She got back on Peggy and gathered the reins. "I don't like it, but I suppose I'll live."

"Course you will." Jesse moved King closer to Peggy. "Bec, look at me."

She shook her head.

"Becky Lee."

She looked. His deep brown eyes appeared sincere, as usual. She quickly lost herself in his gaze. Her heart melted with his soft smile. She was all his. He could do whatever he wanted and she'd be waiting for him when he returned.

"I won't stay out late, I promise. And I'll make it up to you Saturday night. Okay?"

She nodded. She hated the control he had over her.

"It's not the end of the world."

"Maybe not yours," she said under her breath.

Jesse turned his horse toward the embankment. King moved forward a few steps, then Jesse backed him up and looked over his shoulder. "So, Denise will be out tonight?"

"Yeah. Are you gonna hang around?"

Jesse moved King against Peggy. He leaned in toward Becky Lee. "Only if you put a smile back on that pretty face of yours."

She managed a half smile. "Victoria's got a pretty face."

"I don't want to talk about her. I'll race ya back." Jesse cued King, who scampered up the embankment.

Becky Lee watched as her heart was dragged up the hill with Jesse's hand clutched to the rope. There was a void in her that grew worse each time he did something like this. How could she possibly love Jesse McCoy? Probably because she believed that someday all the pain would be worth it. One day he'd give all of himself to her and the void would be filled. Until then, she'd have to be patient.

She drew in a long, deep breath, then remembered that Denise had invited her to go to a party in the city on Friday night. Maybe she should go. Being patient with Jesse didn't mean she had to wait at home while he was out with some other girl. Her heart suddenly felt lighter. Perhaps she'd meet someone new at the party. Then she could make Jesse jealous. That'd get his attention.

Chapter Three

*H*e's going out with someone else tonight?" Becky Lee's best friend, Sarah Moretti, stared at her from across the cafeteria table.

"Yep." She put a spoonful of bland vanilla pudding in her mouth.

"Do you know who he's going out with?"

Becky Lee scooped up another spoonful and turned it upside down. It splattered onto her plate. "What do you suppose is in this stuff? It doesn't even taste like vanilla. What's up with that?"

"What do you expect from school food? Now, come on, Bec, who is it?"

Becky Lee looked around the lunch room. No one sat close enough to hear their conversation in the noisy place. They were all too wrapped up in their own conversations to care anyway. "Her name is Victoria. I think she might be from the city."

"Victoria Spencer?" Sarah said loud enough to turn a few heads.

"I don't know. Who's Victoria Spencer?"

Sarah looked at Becky Lee with wide eyes. "The girl every guy in school has been talking about for the last twenty-four hours. She started here yesterday. Come on, you couldn't have missed her."

"I cut yesterday, remember? I didn't want to deal with Jesse after what happened Wednesday."

"Oh, yeah." Sarah rolled her eyes. "Well, this girl just moved here from the city. Her dad is buying up ranches all over town to put in subdivisions.

He wants to turn Spring Valley into suburbia."

"The girl who came to my house the other day said something about Jesse's family celebrating a real-estate transaction with her family. Does she drive a—"

"Brand new BMW?" Sarah asked.

"Yeah."

Becky Lee's heart sank.

"Hey, ladies."

The two girls looked up. Chris McCoy, Jesse's twin brother, stood beside their table, food tray in hand. Chris and Jesse were identical twins, with the same build and the same dark brown hair and eyes, but totally different personalities.

"Did I interrupt something?" He smiled at Sarah as if he'd just asked her to marry him and was waiting for her to accept.

"Sit down, Chris," Becky Lee said.

Chris sat next to Sarah.

Becky Lee swirled the soda in her cup. "Your brother didn't call me last night to see why I wasn't at school yesterday."

Chris stirred his spaghetti with his fork. "He was busy."

"Doing what?"

Sarah and Chris exchanged a guarded look.

"What are you two hiding?"

"Nothing," Chris replied. "I don't know what he was doing. All I know is he left right after school and got home late."

"He still could have called me."

Chris shrugged. "You know Jesse." He gave a quick laugh.

"Yeah, I do," Becky Lee said. "So, where is he now? I didn't see him in class last period."

Chris stared at his food. "I dunno."

"Yeah, right."

He looked up at her. "Believe me, Becky Lee, you're better off without Jesse."

"You know how many times I've told her that?" Sarah said, pushing her tray off to the side.

Becky Lee knew they were right. But she wasn't ready to admit that to them. "Hey, you two wanna go to the city with me tonight? My sister and her boyfriend are going to a party, and she invited me to go. I'm sure she wouldn't mind if you guys came too."

Sarah's eyes lit up. "Sure, we'll come. Right, Chris?"

Chris nodded eagerly, his mouth full.

"It starts at eight o'clock, so be at my house by seven. We can drive in with my sister."

"Mind if I pick you up?" Chris asked Sarah.

When she agreed, Chris's cheeks flushed and he practically leapt off the seat. Becky Lee stifled a laugh. Chris was such a dork sometimes. But he was a nice dork.

Sarah and Chris kept talking, but Becky Lee stopped listening when she saw Jesse and Victoria walk into the cafeteria. They hung on to each other as if they were holding each other up. They wore sunglasses and were laughing. They just about fell over when they sat down, which made them laugh even more.

Becky Lee let out a small gasp.

Her friends locked into her gaze. "Uh-oh," Sarah and Chris said at the same time.

Becky Lee looked at Chris. "You knew he was with her, didn't you?"

"Well ...yes, but..." Chris stammered.

She stood. "I'm going to find out what they've been up to."

Jesse and Victoria gazed at each other, leaning in close, speaking in hushed tones. Becky Lee approached their table, her arms crossed. They didn't look up. Jesse's leg was stretched out to the side of the table. Becky Lee kicked it hard.

"Ow!" He glared up at her. "What'd you do that for?" he asked as he reached down and rubbed his shin.

"My, don't you two look like you're having a good time?"

Victoria stood and leaned into Becky Lee's face. "What's your problem?"

"What's yours?"

"I don't believe I have one."

"Oh, that's right. People like you don't have problems, do they?"

Victoria planted her hands on her hips. "People like what?"

"Okay, okay!" Jesse stood and pushed between them, his back to Victoria.

Becky Lee saw her reflection in his sunglasses. "Why do you have these on?" She ripped them off and saw his pupils dilated and his eyelids half open. "Jesse McCoy! Have you been smoking pot?"

Victoria stepped in front of Jesse. "If you don't shut your mouth, I'll shut it for you."

"I doubt it. You might break one of those fake nails."

"My nails aren't fake."

Jesse pulled Victoria back. "Stop it, Bec. Vicky hasn't done anything to you."

"Don't tell me what to do."

Sarah came up and grabbed Becky Lee's arm. "Come on, let's go."

Becky Lee pulled her arm back and glared at Sarah.

"Good idea," Victoria said. "Why don't you and your friend just get out of here?"

The threatening tone shot deep into Becky Lee. She clenched her fists, ready for the attack, but Jesse held Victoria by the shoulders.

"You'd better go," he said to Becky Lee.

"Fine." Her eyes locked into his, her voice tense. "But this isn't over." Becky Lee stormed out of the cafeteria, her friend following close behind.

Once outside the cafeteria doors, Sarah said, "You weren't really going to fight her, were you?"

Becky Lee took a deep breath. "I-I don't know." Her voice cracked. "She made me so angry."

"You gonna be all right?"

She half smiled. "Yeah. I'm fine. I'll just walk it off on the way to class."

Becky Lee headed down the hallway. *Going to that party tonight will be good,* she thought. *I'm going to show Jesse McCoy I can get along just fine without him.*

Chapter Four

Becky Lee sat in the backseat of Derek's Camry with Sarah and Chris, watching the team of valet drivers in front of the mansion. Several opened car doors while one took the keys and drove the cars around the back of the enormous house.

"This is so cool!" Becky Lee giggled. "Just like in the movies."

Her sister's boyfriend pulled his car up when the valet motioned him forward.

"So, how do you know the owners of this place?" Becky Lee asked.

Derek glanced at Denise, who sat next to him in the front seat. She shook her head slightly. Derek looked in the rearview mirror. "We're working on a project together."

"What kind of project?" she asked.

Before she could get an answer, a valet was at Denise's door opening it for her. He held out his hand.

Another valet, a gorgeous one, opened Becky Lee's door at the same time. He smiled and extended his hand. Sandy blond hair, piercing blue eyes, and a heart-stopping smile made her feel downright giddy.

"Ma'am?"

Becky Lee giggled again as she stepped out of the car. "You don't have to call me that."

He smiled. "Welcome to the Spencer Estate."

He helped Sarah out next. She giggled too as she slid out. Derek and

Chris had already climbed out on the other side and were standing with Denise gazing up at the mansion.

Becky Lee leaned close to Sarah and whispered, "He was gorgeous!"

"I know," Sarah squealed.

"Did you see him, Denise?" Becky Lee asked.

Denise turned around, "Who?" When Becky Lee rolled her eyes, Denise just laughed and motioned everyone along.

Several concrete steps led up to a massive entryway. Large round pillars lined the edge of the porch, which extended up to a second story. A long, narrow red carpet led from the top of the steps to the oversized double doors. Enormous potted plants flanked the carpet, with an assortment of colored flowers, beautifully accenting the cream-colored exterior.

A woman wearing black slacks, a white shirt, and a black tie met them at the door. "Welcome."

Inside the spacious foyer, several groups of people stood, engaged in conversations and drinking champagne. The men wore tuxedos, and the women wore long dresses. Most of the dresses were black. Some were strapless, some had thin straps, and some were backless. They were all beautiful.

Becky Lee wished she had been able to wear something like that. But the dress she'd borrowed from Denise was nice. She loved how the royal blue brought out the color of her eyes. She liked wearing dresses like this one, with the hem above her knees so her legs had room to walk. Then again, if her dress had slits clear up the thigh, like some of those the other women in the room wore, she wouldn't complain.

Servers dressed in black and white emerged from a hallway beside the staircase, holding trays of champagne glasses and hors d'oeuvres. They worked their way through the crowds of people. When their trays were empty, they returned to the hallway and disappeared behind a door.

Two white columns and a large wooden beam separated the foyer and the next room, where more people stood around visiting. A stage and dance floor headed the front of the room. Round tables covered with white cloths, each with a single red rose in a crystal vase in the center, dotted the middle of the room. Long buffet tables held hot and cold hors d'oeuvres.

Just beyond the tables, a row of windows filled an entire wall from floor to ceiling. Through them Becky Lee saw a lighted patio and a pool. A couple walked in from the patio through French doors and stopped at the bar in the corner of the room.

Denise turned to Becky Lee. "Please stay out of trouble."

"Don't you trust me?"

"Keep an eye on her, Sarah." She smiled, linked her arm through Derek's, and took off.

Becky Lee and Sarah each hooked an arm through one of Chris's, then stuck up their noses.

Chris laughed. "You two are goofy."

As they moved forward, a server walked by with a tray of champagne. Becky Lee grabbed a glass. "This looks good."

"You'll be in trouble if your sister sees you with that." Sarah's face twisted with worry.

"All she can do is take it away. And then I'll just get another one."

Sarah shook her head.

"Besides, holding it makes me feel sophisticated."

Noses up, the three friends entered the main room.

Ballroom music began to play. Several guests made their way to the dance floor.

"Would you like to dance?" Chris asked Sarah.

"I can't dance to classical music."

"Just follow my lead." Chris took Sarah's hand and they walked off. On the dance floor, he raised his right hand and pulled her close with his left. She gave him a puzzled look. He said something in her ear, then she reached up and put her hand in his. The other hand she placed on his shoulder. Chris moved slowly, Sarah following. Becky Lee smiled. What a cute couple.

Becky Lee sipped her champagne, watching Chris and Sarah but also searching the room for cute guys. The only males in this crowd were either with someone or way too old. That was okay. She didn't need to find someone. She just thought it might be fun. Either way, at least she didn't have to worry about fighting with Jesse tonight.

One of the servers approached Becky Lee with a bottle of champagne. "Would you like a refill?"

Noticing her glass was nearly empty, Becky Lee replied, "Yes. Thank you."

She took a long drink, then wove through the crowd toward the hors d'oeuvre table. As she passed by, some people nodded at her; others bade her a "Good evening." Hoping not to reveal herself as an underage drinker, she responded with the same gestures they acknowledged her with. A few older women looked at her with narrowed eyes, but didn't say anything.

Becky Lee scanned the food table from one end to the other. There must have been thirty different kinds of food, from cheeses and wraps to chocolate-dipped strawberries and truffles. Her interest piqued at the sight of a crescent-shaped cracker holding a cupful of little black balls. Curiosity provoked her to reach for one, but she withdrew her hand when a woman came up beside her and took one for herself. Becky Lee watched her take a bite.

"Caviar," the woman said with a satisfied smile. "It's quite good. Try it." She walked off.

Becky Lee picked up the cracker and bit into it. It tasted so horrible she choked. She couldn't wait to get the nasty-tasting thing out of her mouth. She glanced up and down the table, searching for a napkin. They sat at the far end of the table. Nearly gagging from the offensive flavor, she started for the stack, but her path was cut off by a man in a tuxedo.

Looking up she saw the gorgeous guy who'd opened her car door. He stood in front of her, napkin in hand. "Spit it in this before someone sees," he whispered.

Her cheeks getting warm, she took the napkin and spit into it. Her lips twisting with disgust, she drowned the lingering taste with the rest of her champagne. "That was the most awful thing I've ever eaten."

"It's fish eggs," the guy replied with a chuckle. He pointed to the cracker. "You can toss the rest of that into the trash can behind the bar."

Becky Lee followed him to the bar, then slipped behind it to toss the napkin and the rest of the cracker into the garbage receptacle. "Thanks."

"No problem." Mr. Gorgeous winked at Becky Lee.

"Still on duty, Tad?" the bartender asked.

"No. I'm done for the night. I was just about to head home when I saw this lovely lady in need of assistance." Tad smiled at Becky Lee.

She stared at him, mesmerized.

Would you like to dance?" he asked.

"I-I don't know how to dance to this music."

"There's nothing to it." Tad took her hand and led her to the dance floor. Hoping she didn't look as awkward as she felt, she positioned herself the way she'd seen Sarah do and let him take the lead. The beat was slow enough that she could follow. And he was a good dancer. Somehow she managed not to step on his toes.

"Are you from around here?" he asked.

"No," Becky Lee answered, looking at her feet. "I live about an hour out of the city."

"What's your name?"

"Becky Lee Woodson."

"Are you Denise's sister?"

She looked up into his dreamy blue eyes. "Yeah. You know her?"

"I work with her."

"You do?"

"I'm kind of an assistant to the manager at the travel agency, but without management responsibilities."

Becky Lee glanced at his tux.

"This is one of my part-time jobs. Helps me earn a little extra money for college."

"How many jobs do you have?"

"A few. Not all of them are paid work, though. I also volunteer at the hospital a few hours a week."

"How long have you worked at the travel agency?"

"About a year."

"I wonder why Denise never mentioned you. Then again, she never tells me anything. She's always nosing into my business, but I don't know a thing about hers."

Tad flashed a charming smile. "Your sister is probably just being protective of you. I'll bet she's pretty picky about the guys you go out with."

"Oh, she tries to control me, but it's no use. I date whoever I want to."

"Sore subject, huh? Is she interfering in one of your relationships?"

"The only relationship I've ever been in. Or was in, I should say."

Becky Lee fell silent. She didn't want to talk about Jesse. As Tad continued to lead her, she gazed over his shoulder, searching the room for her friends. She wanted them to see that she was dancing with this gorgeous guy.

She saw Sarah at the buffet tables, putting food on a small plate. Chris stood a few feet from her, talking to some guy whose back was to Becky Lee. Her eyes met Chris's. He pointed to her, and the guy turned around.

It was Jesse.

Becky Lee stopped dancing.

"Is something wrong?" Tad followed her gaze.

Jesse's face tightened. Anger flashed in his eyes. His glare pierced her heart. Shaking his head, he walked off.

Tad looked back at Becky Lee. "Who was that?"

"No one. I could use a refill. Do you mind?" Without waiting for an answer, Becky Lee rushed toward the bar. A tray of glasses sat on the counter. She helped herself to one and drank its contents all at once.

What was Jesse doing here? He was supposed to be at a celebration with Victoria's family.

She'd just grabbed another glass of champagne when Tad came up beside her. "Are you all right?"

"Yeah."

"You should take it easy on that stuff." He nodded at her glass.

"Don't lecture me."

Tad held up his hands. "Sorry."

"Who's throwing this party?" she shot out.

"Mr. and Mrs. Spencer. They just bought a ranch outside of town and are celebrating—"

"No way," Becky Lee interrupted. "I'm at Victoria Spencer's party?" She downed her champagne. "I need another drink."

"I don't think that's a good idea." Tad took her glass.

Becky Lee spoke through clenched teeth. "Don't tell me what to do."

"How about we go outside? Cool off for a few minutes."

Becky Lee hesitated. Her gut reaction told her to tell this guy to take a hike. But for some reason, she allowed him to lead her through the French doors.

The fresh air felt cool on her face. She drew in a long breath. Her anger gave way to numbness.

As she crossed the cement patio, she stumbled. Tad caught her arm. He helped her down several steps to the path that led to the lighted pool. He guided her to an empty table and pulled out a chair for her.

Becky Lee fell into the chair and stared at the pool and the rock waterfall that graced one end of it. "It would be fun to slide down that."

Tad sat next to her and glanced at the waterfall. "I don't think those big rocks would feel too good." He grinned at Becky Lee.

She smiled back. Propping her elbow on the arm of the chair, she rested her head in her palm. Her body swayed slightly back and forth. She slipped and fell forward. Tad reached for her, but she caught herself before falling out of the chair.

"Oops!" She laughed and righted herself.

"You're pretty hammered." Tad's tone sounded serious but gentle. She detected no judgment in his statement. "Do you do this often?"

"No, no, no. I can handle my alcohol just fine. In fact, I'd like some more." She lowered her chin and looked up at him like a puppy. "Pretty please?"

"Maybe in a little bit. I'd like to talk for a while first."

Becky Lee shrugged.

Tad leaned forward, resting his elbows on his knees. "Was that guy your boyfriend?"

"No."

"Who is he?"

"What business is it of yours?" She leaned back in the chair and crossed her arms.

"It's not. I'd just like to help if I can."

"Well, you can't. So just forget about it, okay? Can I have some more champagne now?"

"No," Tad answered, his voice soft.

"Then I'll get it myself." She stood and pressed the creases out of her dress. She took one step and tripped over her feet. Tad jumped out of his seat and steadied her. She put her hand against her throbbing head.

"Still think you need more?"

"My mouth is dry."

"How about some water?"

"Okay." She figured she'd let him take her back inside, then ditch him so she could get more champagne.

Once inside, she sat in a chair next to the wall of windows. Tad went to the bar and spoke to the bartender. Becky Lee looked for an opportunity to escape.

The crowd grew quiet. Everyone faced the stage.

A guitar played music she recognized. After several notes, she heard Jesse's voice singing a song he had written for her. She looked toward the stage, but too many people stood in front of her. She kicked off her shoes, placed her hands on the window to balance herself, and climbed onto the chair.

On the stage, Victoria sat on a stool next to Jesse. Their eyes locked on each other. He sang Becky Lee's song to Victoria.

"How dare he!"

A couple standing at the buffet tables glanced at Becky Lee, then looked away.

Tad came up beside her, holding a glass of water. "What's wrong?" he whispered.

"I'm not gonna let him get away with this." She scrambled off the chair and shoved her feet back into her shoes.

"Becky Lee, stay here." Tad grabbed her arm and pulled her back. She lost her balance and fell into him. The glass he held tilted, and water spilled down the front of her dress.

Becky Lee gasped as the cold liquid seeped through her dress and ran down her bare legs. "Look what you did."

"I'm sorry. Let's get you a towel."

As they left the room, Becky Lee looked back at the stage. She caught a glimpse of Jesse watching her, but still singing. She stopped and held his gaze for a moment. Rage welled up in her heart.

She heard Tad talking with someone in the foyer. Then he was beside her, his hand on her shoulder. "Come on."

She pretended to lose her balance and let herself fall into Tad's arms. He wrapped her in an embrace to help steady her. She looked deeply into his eyes and took his hand.

She turned back to Jesse, smirked at him, then strutted out of the room.

In the foyer, Tad pulled his hand away from Becky Lee and pointed up the stairs. "First door on the left is a guest room. There are towels in the bathroom."

"Aren't you going to come with me?"

"I don't think that's necessary."

"Oh, come on, Tad. Don't you want to make sure I don't fall down the stairs?" She winked. "Or sneak some more champagne?"

"There's no champagne up there."

"Please?" she begged.

Tad hesitated, then gave in. "Okay."

They went upstairs and opened the bedroom door. Becky Lee stepped inside. Tad stayed in the hallway. "Aren't you coming in?" she asked.

"No. I'm going to go find your sister." Tad walked back toward the stairs.

Becky Lee shook her head. "Jerk!"

She went into the bathroom, flipped on the light, and shut the door. The huge bathroom had emerald green sinks, counter, commode, shower stall, and sunken tub.

She pulled a white towel off the rod and dabbed at her dress. She reached down to wipe her legs, but as soon as she bent over, the room started to spin. She straightened, using the counter to steady herself. She looked in the mirror. Her vision blurred. Her stomach clenched. She grabbed the edge of the tub, sat down, and held her head in her hands.

A knock sounded on the bedroom door. "Becky Lee, are you all right?" Sarah's voice brought relief.

"Yeah. Come in."

Sarah opened the door and came into the bathroom, her eyes wide and her face serious. "What are you doing up here? And what were you doing with that guy? Did he try anything with you?"

Becky Lee managed a sarcastic laugh. "I wish. But he had no interest in me."

Sarah grabbed a washcloth and ran it under a stream of water in the sink.

"I had a little too much champagne. And all of sudden this guy Tad starts acting like he's my guardian angel or something. First he wouldn't let me have any more to drink, then he stopped me from causing a scene when Jesse was serenading what's-her-face. I was about ready to rip out Jesse's vocal cords when Tad grabbed me and spilled water on my dress."

Sarah turned off the water and wrung out the cloth.

"Where's Chris?" Becky Lee asked.

"Talking to Jesse. I saw you come up here with that guy, then he came back downstairs without you. I wanted to make sure you were all right. Jesse saw you too."

"With Victoria hanging off his arm?"

"Actually, she was hitting on Chris while Jesse and I were talking."

"What? I'm going down there to tell her what I think of her." Becky Lee started to stand, but Sarah eased her back down.

"Not a good idea." Sarah handed the cloth to Becky Lee. "You're not looking so good."

Becky Lee put the cloth over her face and leaned against the green tub. "I'm not feeling so good either."

"Don't worry about Victoria right now."

Becky Lee pulled the cloth away. "Do I look like I'm worried?"

"No, it looks like you're hurting."

The bedroom door slammed open. Jesse stormed into the bathroom doorway, anger in his eyes. "I need to talk with Becky Lee."

Sarah put a hand on Jesse's chest. "Now is not a good time."

"Chris is in the hallway waiting for you."

Sarah looked at Becky Lee, her eyes silently asking what she wanted her to do.

Becky Lee shrugged.

"I'll be right outside if you need me." Sarah shot a glare at Jesse and walked out, shutting the bedroom door behind her. Jesse grabbed Becky Lee by the arm and jerked her from the bathroom into the bedroom. He shoved her onto the bed.

She sat on the edge, her fists latched onto the bedspread, trying to keep from swaying. "You can't come in here and start pushing me around."

Jesse stood in front of her, his teeth clenched. "What are you doing at this party?"

Becky Lee looked up at Jesse. Her vision blurred again. She squeezed her eyes shut, then reopened them. They refocused. "I was invited."

"And what were you doing in here with that guy?"

Jenn A. Sesto

"What do you care? You were down there singing your heart out to what's-her-face, right in front of me." Tears rimmed her eyes. "The song you wrote for me."

Jesse backed off a bit. "She asked me to sing tonight. You know that's the only song I have finished right now. I didn't know she was going to sit up there with me."

"You could have told her no."

Jesse sighed. His face softened. He looked at the floor, then back at Becky Lee. He sat beside her. "I know you've been mad at me. When I saw you come up here with that guy, I thought you might do something to try to hurt me."

"If I did, that'd be none of your business, now, would it?"

Jesse put his arms around her and pulled her close. "Guess I screwed up by coming here tonight, huh?"

She crumpled in his arms and let the tears fall.

"I'm sorry," he said.

She looked up at him. "Why don't you make it up to me?" She kissed his soft, warm lips.

His eyes closed. He kissed her back. Between kisses, he whispered, "Vicky."

Becky Lee pushed him back and stumbled off the bed. "What did you just call me?"

He jumped up and reached for her. "I wasn't calling you Vicky. I was just thinking it wouldn't be right for us to do something in somebody else's house."

Becky Lee backed up. "That's never stopped you before."

"I don't feel right about it."

"You're just worried she might catch you. But it wouldn't matter if I caught you with her, would it?"

He gave no answer.

"I'm tired of running in circles, Jes." She covered her face with her hands and sobbed.

Jesse pulled her into his arms. "I know, Bec. I'm sorry."

She pushed him away and wiped her face. "You should be, but I know you don't mean it. If we make up tonight, you'll be doing the same thing all over again next week."

The bedroom door slammed open and hit the wall. A large man entered the room.

"Mr. Spencer?" Jesse stammered.

He looked from Becky Lee to Jesse. "What's going on in here?"

Victoria squeezed between her daddy and the doorway, a cocky smile on her lips.

"It's not what you think, sir," Jesse said.

"We were just talking," Becky Lee added.

"It's all right, Daddy. Jesse is with me." Victoria latched onto Jesse's arm. "And she was just leaving. Right, Jesse?"

"Yes, sir," he said without a glance at Becky Lee.

Her heart wilted.

Mr. Spencer smiled at his daughter. "Okay, Vicky. Now, I've got guests to attend to. Don't interrupt me again." He left the room.

Becky Lee felt the room spin even more than before. The floor seemed to move beneath her.

"Come on, Jesse." Victoria pulled him out of the room. He didn't even look back.

Tears welled up in Becky Lee's eyes. She slunk back onto the bed.

Sarah appeared in the doorway. "Are you okay?" she asked, racing to her side.

Becky Lee choked on a sob. "I need to find my sister."

The room went black.

Chapter Five

The phone rang. Becky Lee pulled her pillow over her head, trying to block out the annoying sound. She knew who it would be, but she didn't want to speak to him. She just wanted to sleep. Her head hurt from drinking too much last night.

The phone kept ringing. Groaning, she pulled off the pillow and reached for the cordless phone on her night stand. She pushed the Talk button.

"What?" she grumbled into the phone.

"Hi," came Jesse's chipper voice on the other end. "Were you sleeping?"

"Yeah. Do you mind?"

"I thought maybe we could go to the river. You know, to our special spot."

"Well, you thought wrong." Becky Lee hung up. She pulled the covers over her head and closed her eyes.

A knock sounded. The door opened. Denise poked her head inside. "How are you feeling?"

"Peachy."

Denise came in and sat on the edge of the bed. She gently pulled the blankets from Becky Lee's face. "I'm sorry about last night."

"It's not your fault." Becky Lee covered her eyes with her forearm. "You didn't know Jesse was gonna be there." She moved her arm and looked at

Jenn A. Sesto

Denise. "Is Mr. Spencer your buyer for the ranch?"

"Yes. But he knows I want to wait until you graduate."

"Is Derek designing the new homes the Spencers are building?"

"Yeah. Pretty cool, huh?"

"Will you get me some aspirin, please."

Denise moved to the door. "Champagne's the worst for hangovers."

"Now you tell me."

She paused in the doorway. "Want some breakfast?"

"I don't think I could eat anything right now."

"Okay. I'll be right back with aspirin and water." She shut the door behind her.

The phone rang again.

Becky Lee picked up. "Hello?"

"Is this Becky Lee?" a deep voice asked.

"Yeah. Who's this?"

"It's Tad."

The valet driver and guardian angel. "How'd you get my number?"

"You gave it to me. Don't you remember?"

"I did not!"

Tad laughed. "I'm kidding. Your sister gave it to me. I told her I wanted to check on you today. See how you were doing. I hope you don't mind."

"No, I don't. Actually I thought you'd be mad at me."

"Why?"

"From what I remember, I wasn't the best person to be around last night."

"You were upset. And alcohol only intensifies things."

"I'm sure I embarrassed you."

"It takes a lot to embarrass me." He chuckled. "So, what are you doing today?"

"Nothing."

"Well, I'm going down to the river. I have to write a term paper, and

I know a place that's quiet and peaceful. I do a lot of my studying there. Would you like to go with me?"

"Sure." She cringed at how quickly she'd responded.

"I'll pick you up in an hour."

"Make it an hour and a half."

"You got it. And I'll pack a lunch. But I need directions to your house."

Becky Lee rattled off directions, then said good-bye.

She sat up too quickly. *Oh, my head!* Where was Denise with that aspirin?

At her sister's suggestion, Becky Lee took a warm bath after swallowing the pills. She soon felt like her usual self again. Except for one thing.

She couldn't remember ever feeling this excited about going out with Jesse. There was something different about Tad. She didn't know what, but she couldn't wait to find out.

❦ ❦ ❦

After her bath, Becky Lee put on her swimsuit and shorts and headed downstairs. She found Denise in the kitchen, sitting at the table. She was reading the newspaper, sipping a cup of coffee, and eating toast. She looked up when Becky Lee entered the room.

"Feeling better?"

"Yeah." Becky Lee pulled out a piece of bread and popped it into the toaster. She leaned against the counter.

"Why are you in your swimsuit?"

"I'm going to the river."

"With Jesse?" Denise took a bite of her toast.

"No. With Tad."

"Tad O'Neill?" Denise choked on her toast.

"Is something wrong?" Becky Lee asked.

"No. That's great. I...I think he's exactly what you need right now." She grinned.

Becky Lee's eyes narrowed. "Now, don't be thinking Jesse's out of the picture. Even though I'm mad at him right now, I still love him."

Denise stood and poured herself more coffee. "Want some?"

Becky Lee shook her head.

Denise set the carafe back on the burner. "I think you'll like Tad. He's very different from Jesse."

The doorbell sounded. Denise smiled. "Why don't you answer it?"

Becky Lee shook her head and left the kitchen. Butterflies swarmed in her stomach as she opened the front door.

"Jesse!"

"Where you going?" he asked, looking at her swimsuit.

"To the river."

"I thought you didn't want to go."

"I didn't when I talked to you."

"Can I come in?"

"Yeah, I guess."

As he strolled into the living room, she looked out at the road. No cars were coming. She turned to Jesse and leaned against the door. "What do you want?"

Jesse took her hands in his. "I'm really sorry for last night. It was a mistake for me to go to that party."

"What's the matter? Victoria tell you never to call her again?"

"This has nothing to do with her. I really am sorry."

"Don't worry, I'm over it." Becky Lee pulled her hands away.

"I want to make it up to you."

"I told you, I'm going to the river today."

"I know. But maybe tonight we can go out. I'll take you to dinner."

Becky Lee shifted on her feet. "I don't know what time I'll be back."

"I'll wait for you." Jesse kissed her cheek and pushed the screen door open. "Call me when you get home."

"You gonna wait all day for me to call?"

"Yeah." Jesse stepped out onto the porch, but stopped cold when he

Sweet Surrender

saw Tad walking up the path.

Jesse turned back to Becky Lee and kissed her on the lips. "Call me when you get back from the river. I'll be waiting." He walked across the porch and down the steps. At the bottom, Jesse stopped and exchanged looks with Tad. Then he headed down the driveway.

Tad came up to the door. "Was this bad timing?"

"No. He's just being weird." In her heart, however, Becky Lee wondered why Jesse seemed so calm when he saw Tad. "Come in for a sec. I need to grab my bag."

Tad stepped inside. Becky Lee shut the door behind him.

"Denise is in there." She pointed toward the kitchen. "I'll be back down in a minute."

Tad strolled into the kitchen. Becky Lee heard him talking to her sister. Anticipation welled up in her as she ran up the stairs.

❦ ❦ ❦

Becky Lee followed Tad along a path in the middle of some thick, tall brush. He was several steps ahead of her.

"You doing okay?" he asked over his shoulder.

"Yeah, I'm fine. How much farther?"

"Not much. Is that picnic basket too heavy?"

"I got it. What did you pack?"

"I wasn't sure what you like, so I brought a bunch of things. Do you want me to carry it?"

"No." He already had two chairs, a blanket, and his backpack. She hadn't thought he was serious about doing homework at the river.

Tad stopped. Becky Lee came up behind him.

"What do you think?" he asked.

She looked around the secluded clearing. A small, sandy beach met the river's edge. The tall brush they had just walked through outlined the area. It grew over the river at the east and west ends, making it look like just a lone swimming hole. At the west end, a huge rock sat partially on the beach and partly in the water.

"No one would ever know we were here." She set the basket down. "How did you find this place?"

Tad unloaded the chairs and blanket on the beach. "This part of the river flows through my family's property."

If this was his family property, how did she not know him before now?

Tad opened the two chairs and spread the blanket out on the sand. He set the picnic basket on the blanket, then tossed his backpack on one of the chairs. He motioned Becky Lee to the blanket. "Want something to drink? I have soda and water."

"Water, please." Becky Lee knelt down.

He handed her a plastic bottle. "I can put the food out now if you'd like."

"I'm not really hungry at the moment."

"Okay." Tad grabbed a water bottle for himself, then sat next to her.

Becky Lee twisted off the cap and took a sip. "So, this is your family's property?"

Tad chuckled. "Close to three hundred and eighty acres. It belonged to my great-grandparents. Unfortunately, my parents had to have the house torn down about three years ago, when my grandfather died. He was ninety-eight."

That explained how he could have property here, but she didn't know him.

"The house was falling apart so badly that when my parents looked into fixing it up, the county told them it needed to be condemned. It would've cost more money to bring it up to code than it would be worth. My folks might rebuild and retire here. They've offered to let me build on it someday, too, whenever I decide to settle down."

"That's cool." Becky Lee slipped into fantasy mode. "Can you imagine how many horses and cattle you could have here? What an awesome ranch you'd have."

"I'm no rancher. I've never even been on a horse."

"How sad." She shook her head.

"Actually," he said with a chuckle, "I rode a pony once at the county fair. I was around five. My dad tried to help me on the animal, but I insisted on doing it myself. I swung my leg over so fast, I went off on the other side."

Becky Lee roared. "That must have been hilarious."

"My parents thought it was pretty comical, once they knew I wasn't hurt. I never did ride that pony. I was too embarrassed to get back on."

"You'll have to come over someday and ride with me."

"I'm not really anxious to get on a horse."

"Are you afraid?" she teased.

He gave a sheepish look. "A little intimidated."

Tad's sensitivity to horses sparked a soft note in her heart. She liked that he admitted he was afraid of something. Not cocky, like Jesse. "So, how many years have you been afraid of horses?"

"I'm twenty-one now, so about sixteen years, I guess. How old are you?"

"I'll be eighteen in a couple of weeks."

"Then you're graduating this year?"

"Hopefully."

Tad raised his eyes in question.

"I have some catching up to do. Grades are little low right now."

Tad smiled. "Any plans for college?"

"No. I'd like to get my daddy's ranch going again. If Denise doesn't sell it. We used to breed and sell cows. And some horses. But Denise had to sell everything, except two of the horses, to help pay bills after my parents died."

"I'm sorry about your folks."

Becky Lee looked away. A touch of sadness still weighed on her heart.

"So your sister doesn't want to keep the ranch, huh?"

"No. Her boyfriend is from the city. That's where she wants to be too.

Jenn A. Sesto

The only reason she's stayed this long is because of me. She's planning on selling to Mr. Spencer once I finish school."

"He seems to be buying up everything on your side of town."

"I wish there was some way I could afford to keep the ranch." Becky Lee took another sip of water. She wouldn't mind putting a damper on Mr. Spencer's suburbia plans.

"Maybe you can buy property somewhere else someday."

"I don't want to leave this town. It's all I know." She sighed. "I'd expected Jesse to help me out, but now . . ."

"Were you two planning on getting married?"

"Maybe at some point. We figured we'd live together first to see if things worked out."

"Living together doesn't guarantee a marriage will succeed. It just makes it easier to walk away."

"Well, I don't want to get divorced."

"I don't believe in divorce or living together before marriage." Tad reached for his backpack. "Mind if I work on my paper for a while?"

Becky Lee shrugged and lay back on the blanket. She closed her eyes. As she listened to him rummage through his things, she wondered what was up with this guy. *He's so old-fashioned.* He'd probably end up divorced before she would.

She opened her eyes and squinted at the sun. She turned her head slightly, but all she saw was brush. She sat up, wondering if he had left her alone. Then she saw him, sitting on a large rock by the water. A book lay open in his lap, but he wasn't reading it. He was looking up, his eyes closed, his hands folded. His lips were moving, but no sound came out of his mouth. He lowered his head, eyes still closed.

"Tad?"

He looked over.

"What are you doing?"

"Praying."

"What?"

48

"I always pray before I study."

"You do?"

He nodded.

"Okay. Sorry for interrupting."

"No problem." Tad smiled. He closed his eyes again.

Becky Lee lay back down and closed her eyes. She thought it weird that he would pray right there in front of her. She felt a little nervous, though she didn't know why. She'd never felt the need to pray. She didn't know how. She'd never even been to church.

Oh, well. One thing was for sure. She was definitely not his type.

❦ ❦ ❦

"Becky Lee." Tad nudged her shoulder.

It took her a moment to remember where she was. She blinked a few times, then realized that the sun had moved. She jumped up. "What time is it?"

"About five-thirty."

Becky Lee took a deep breath. "I've been sleeping this whole time?"

"Since about three."

"Why didn't you wake me?"

"I got wrapped up in my paper and wasn't paying attention to the time."

Becky Lee felt embarrassed. "I hope I didn't snore."

Tad smiled. "I didn't hear any snoring."

"Good. Jesse says I snore real loud."

Tad's smile disappeared.

"What's wrong?"

Tad folded up a chair. "Nothing."

Becky Lee stood and grabbed the other chair. "Sorry. I'm sure you don't want to hear about me and Jesse."

"I just think it's sad."

"What?"

"How common it is for people these days to have sex before they get married." Tad picked up the blanket, shook it out, and started folding it.

Becky Lee stood there, stunned. "That's what you do when you've gone out with someone for a long time."

"Exactly. It has become routine, no big deal." Tad set the blanket on top of the basket and faced Becky Lee. "I don't believe in premarital sex."

Becky Lee's eyes widened. "What are you, some kind of saint or something?"

"If you knew Jesus Christ the way I do, you'd see things differently."

"So you're a Christian," she said with a hint of sarcasm in her voice. "Does that mean you can't date or have a girlfriend?"

"I have a lot of girls who are friends, and we do things in groups."

"If you don't date, how will you know when you've found the right one?"

"The Lord will bring that special person to me when the time is right. Our paths will cross when it's His time, not my time."

Becky Lee picked up her water bottle from the sand. "Have you ever wanted to …you know, be with someone?"

Tad's face softened. "Once, when I was a senior in high school, there was a girl I really liked. Just as I started to think she might be the one, her family moved away. I haven't heard from her since. So it wasn't meant to be. It's not what God wanted for me."

"That's it? You just gave up?"

He shrugged.

Becky Lee did not understand this guy. If she and Jesse broke up, she'd find someone else. She couldn't imagine not having a boyfriend for a long period of time. "What about college?" she asked. "Anyone special there?"

Tad shook his head. "I'm pretty wrapped up in my studies."

"What are you studying?"

"After I graduate, I plan to go into ministry. Be a pastor."

Becky Lee laughed. "Then I'm sure not the kind of person you should be with. I'm not even a Christian."

Tad smiled. "I just want to be your friend. That's all."

"I've already got a best friend. Sarah."

"I know. But I can be your friend, too, right?"

She shrugged. "I guess."

"It's going to be dark soon. We need to head home."

Becky Lee grabbed the picnic basket and blanket. As she followed Tad back down the path, she wondered about her new friend. Why would a guy want to be just friends with a girl? There wasn't one guy at school who didn't have a girlfriend or was on the prowl for one. But Tad was different.

What did he see in her? Why did he pick her out a crowd of people at a party? Then invite her to hang out at the river while he studied? There had to be some other reason than just wanting to be her friend. She resolved to find out why.

Chapter Six

ecky Lee called Jesse after she returned from the river, but his brother Chris said he wasn't home. So much for taking her dinner. Apparently, he'd forgotten all about it.

For the next two weeks, he ignored her. Every time she saw Jesse at school, he was with Victoria. They'd pass in the hallway and he wouldn't even make eye contact with her. It was like she didn't exist.

They had never been split up this long. She wondered whether he would come back to her this time. If he did, would she take him back?

Tad, on the other hand, had been hanging out with Becky Lee a lot. He offered to help her with homework, saying he was pretty good at algebra, which was one of the subjects she was failing. They'd met at her house several times after school.

Denise was so glad that Becky Lee wasn't around Jesse, and that she was finally focused on her school work, she cooked dinner for Tad every time he was there.

Becky Lee had never met anyone like Tad. He was sweet and sensitive. She liked being his friend. She even allowed herself to fantasize about what it would be like to be his girlfriend. She wondered if he would hold her hand or kiss her without being married. He'd made his no-dating rule clear, but what other rules were there?

He seemed completely into his God, and God made the rules. So why would he be interested in being friends with a non-religious person?

Becky Lee was sitting on her bed, daydreaming about Tad, when Sarah burst into the room. "Happy eighteenth birthday," she squealed.

Her birthday wasn't till the next day, but Denise had planned a special dinner for her that night. So Sarah and Becky Lee were going to celebrate tonight. Zack, a guy from school, and his college-aged brother were throwing a party while their parents were out of town. Plenty of drinking, dancing, and loud music. Becky Lee could hardly wait.

"How do I look?" Sarah strutted up and down the room as if she were in a fashion show. She wore a black miniskirt and a black satin tank top. Rhinestones along the neckline sparkled in the overhead light. She spun around and stopped, then paraded to other end of the bed and spun again, but this time lost her balance. She bounced on the bed, then fell to the floor.

"Are you all right?" Becky Lee asked.

Sarah pushed herself up, laughing so hard she couldn't speak.

Becky Lee burst out in laughter too.

Denise entered the room, the cordless phone in her hand. "It's Jesse."

Becky Lee stopped laughing.

"I'll tell him you don't want to talk to him if you want."

"No." She took the phone from her sister.

After Denise left the room, Becky Lee took a deep breath. "Hello?"

"Hey, Bec. How are ya?" Jesse's voice was casual, as if nothing had happened.

"Fine."

"You going to Zack's party tonight?"

"Sarah and I are going out," she said, wanting him to be surprised when he saw her there. She wondered if he remembered that tomorrow was her birthday. "I suppose we might stop by later."

"Okay. Well, maybe I'll see you there."

"Maybe. Bye." Becky Lee pushed the Off button and threw the phone on the bed.

"What did he say?" Sarah asked.

"He might be at Zack's party tonight."

"Is Victoria going to be there?"

"I don't know." Becky Lee's heart quickened. "Do you think Jesse wants to get back together with me?"

"No way. I won't let you."

"But what if he broke up with Victoria and wants me back?"

"What about Tad?"

"We're just friends."

"Then you need to look for someone else. Steer clear of Jesse McCoy."

Becky Lee looked at the clock. "Oh, my gosh, the party has already started. Throw me my dress."

Sarah reached for the red mini-dress that hung on the closet door. She tossed it onto the bed. Becky Lee threw the garment over head and adjusted the thin straps over her shoulders.

"Where are my shoes?"

"Right here." Sarah picked up the red high heels off the floor and handed them to Becky Lee.

She slipped on her shoes, grabbed Sarah's hand, and led her outside, giggling all the way.

"Look," Sarah said as she climbed into the driver's seat of her Escort, "I'm serious. I want you to stay away from Jesse tonight."

Becky Lee smirked. "Easier said than done."

❧ ❧ ❧

"There's a spot." Becky Lee pointed to a small open space between a jacked-up four-wheel drive and a late-model Mustang. It looked barely big enough for Sarah to pull into.

After parallel parking, the girls strutted down the street to Zack's house. Several people hung out on the front lawn, drinking beer. Becky Lee recognized some of them from school, but most looked college age.

The two girls stepped inside the house. People were packed into the kitchen off to the right and in the living room to the left.

Becky Lee hooked arms with Sarah and shouted over the country music. "Let's go over there." She nodded toward the far corner of the living room, where several kegs lined the wall. Two guys were filling cups and handing them out.

Sarah squeezed Becky Lee's arm. "Don't let go of me."

Becky Lee pushed through the crowded living room. "I'll take two, please," she said.

The guy holding the keg nozzle cupped his hand over his ear. She held up two fingers. He filled a glass and handed it to Sarah, then filled a second one. As he handed it to her, he asked, "Aren't you Becky Lee Woodson?"

"Maybe," she flirted. "Who are you?"

"Danny McCoy," he shouted. "Jesse's cousin. Don't you remember me?"

She shook her head. Then it came to her. "The reunion last summer, right?"

Danny nodded. "I'm visiting friends this weekend."

"Cool." When Sarah elbowed her, she added, "This is my best friend, Sarah."

"Nice to meet you," Danny said with a smile that reminded Becky Lee too much of Jesse's.

Becky Lee took a swig of her beer. "How come you and Chris got all the manners?"

Danny motioned Becky Lee closer. "Chris told me you and Jesse aren't together anymore?"

She shook her head.

"Maybe we could get together sometime this weekend."

Her smile widened. "Maybe."

Glancing at the long beer line that had formed behind the girls, Danny said, "We'll talk more later." He resumed filling cups, and Becky Lee and Sarah moved across the room. They hung out between the kitchen and living room, watching people talk, drink, and dance.

"Isn't Tad worried that someone's gonna whisk you away?" came a voice from behind her.

Becky Lee turned to find Jesse, flashing his charming smile.

Her legs weakened. Her heart skipped a beat. Refusing to let him know what was going on inside her, she said casually, "Oh, hi, Jes. How are you?"

"I'm fine. Now that I've got Vicky off my hands."

Becky Lee caught her breath. A burst of hope flared inside her.

Jesse looked around. "Are you here alone?

"I'm her date." Sarah put her arm around Becky Lee. The girls giggled. Jesse's face reddened.

"I'm not here with a guy, if that's what you mean." Becky Lee took another drink of her beer.

"Can we talk?"

"No." Sarah's serious tone left no room for argument.

Becky Lee shot Sarah a pleading look. "We're just gonna talk."

Sarah grabbed her arm. "No."

The loud rock music changed to a slow song.

"Let's dance," Jesse said.

Becky Lee put her hand in his. Sarah gasped. "It'll be fine," Becky Lee assured her.

Jesse led her into the living room and pulled her close. His cheek touched hers. She closed her eyes and sank into his arms.

No! She wouldn't give in that easily. She put a slight distance between them. "So, what did you want to talk about?"

"What's going on between you and Tad?" Jesse asked.

So, *he* was jealous of *her* for a change. That was a switch.

"I've noticed his car at your house quite a bit over the last couple of weeks."

"So?"

Jesse's jaw tightened. "Are you seeing him?"

"Yes." She'd let him draw his own conclusion. After all, she *was* seeing him...just not the way he might think.

The corners of Jesse's mouth pulled down. "I'm so sorry, Bec. I've been a real jerk lately."

The famous apology, always so sincere sounding. It had been the breaking point for her more times than she could count.

"Can we go somewhere? So we can talk in private?"

"I-I don't think so."

"Please, Bec."

The desperation in his voice penetrated her heart. But she had to stay strong. "We can talk here."

Jesse shook his head. "Let's go back to my house. No one's home."

An alarm went off in her head. She pulled out of his grip. "I need to stay with Sarah."

"We'll come back."

Becky Lee hesitated. She knew she would not be able to withstand him if he got her alone.

"We'll be back within an hour. I promise."

One hour? Maybe that would be okay. She paused. "All right. Let me go tell Sarah."

A look of triumph sparkled in Jesse's eyes. "My truck is out front. I'll wait for you there."

Becky Lee found Sarah by the kegs, talking with Danny. "I'm leaving with Jesse."

Sarah's eyebrows rose. "What?"

"We'll be back in an hour. Maybe less."

"Yeah right."

"I promise."

Sarah flailed her arms. "This was supposed to be a girls night out. If I knew you were going to run off with Jesse—"

"I'm not. We're just going to talk. I'll be right back."

Sarah rolled her eyes.

"Trust me." Becky Lee leaned over to Danny. "Give her some more beer so she'll lighten up, okay?"

He smiled and nodded. Becky headed for the front door before Sarah could protest any more.

"I'm calling you in one hour if you're not back," Sarah yelled after her.

Becky Lee waved over her shoulder as she made her way through the crowd. She could hardly wait to hear what Jesse had to say to her.

❦ ❦ ❦

Becky Lee's stomach tightened as Jesse unlocked the door to his house. She hoped she wasn't making a mistake. They were just going to talk, she told herself, and that was it. They'd be back at the party in less than an hour. She'd watch the clock to make sure.

Jesse locked the door behind them. Leaving the lights off, he took her hand.

"So, where are your parents?"

"They're gone for the weekend."

"Where's Chris?"

"He's with them. We have the house to ourselves."

He started for the stairs. "Come up to my room. I want to show you something."

Becky Lee stood her ground. "I thought we were just gonna talk."

"We will."

When they got to his room, Jesse turned on the light. He pointed to the bed. "Sit down."

She sat on the edge of the bed.

Jesse pulled out his chair from under the desk and set it facing Becky Lee. Then he grabbed his guitar, which had been leaning against the wall. "I want you to hear the new song I wrote." He sat in front of her. "I've been writing quite a bit over the last couple of weeks."

He glanced at the strings and played a few notes, then looked back at

Becky Lee. Gazing into her eyes, he sang a beautiful love song about a guy and a girl who were in love but had relationship problems. The guy wanted to work it out, but the girl wasn't sure.

Becky Lee's eyes misted. She tried to blink back the tears.

When he stopped playing, he kissed her on the forehead. "Well?"

"It's beautiful."

"I met someone at Victoria's party."

Becky Lee's heart dropped.

"A music producer. He heard me sing at the party and asked for a demo tape. So I'm making one. I'm going to Nashville week after next."

"Nashville?"

Jesse leaned the guitar against the bed. He cupped Becky Lee's face in his hands. "I want you to come with me."

"What?"

"Denise is going to sell your ranch soon. Why not move out a little early?"

"What about school?"

"I can't wait till school's over. This guy wants me now, as soon as the tape is ready."

"But we graduate in three months."

Jesse leaned back in the chair. "When did you get all righteous about school?"

Becky Lee lowered her head. "I don't know. I'm sorry. I didn't mean to take away from your excitement. But we've got to finish school."

Jesse raked his hands through his hair and sighed. "I ain't graduating in June. I failed too many classes. I'd have to do summer school plus another semester." He took her hands in his. "If I tell this guy he has to wait another six months, I'll lose this opportunity. And if I make it big, who cares whether I graduate?"

Becky Lee stared into Jesse's eyes. She desperately wanted to say yes, but she couldn't leave. Not now. "I thought we were going to try to get my father's ranch operating again."

Jesse squeezed her hands. "There's no way we could make that work."

"But that's my dream."

"And this is mine."

Becky Lee drew in a deep breath. She knew she would not be able to stop him. "Then go."

"What about you?"

"Let me think about it, okay?"

"Okay. Just remember I love you."

"I love you too."

Just as Jesse bent close to kiss her, Becky Lee's cell phone rang. She reached for her purse on the bed beside her.

Jesse put his hand on hers. "Don't answer it."

She pulled the phone out on the third ring. It was Sarah. Had it been an hour already? "Hey, girl."

"Where are you?"

"I'm still with Jesse."

"You were supposed to be back here by now."

Becky Lee lost herself in Jesse's gaze. "We'll just be a little bit longer."

Jesse grabbed the phone. "I'll have her back soon. Don't worry." He hung up and pushed the Silent Mode button.

His arrogance struck a wrong chord in Becky Lee. She reached for her phone, but he held it behind him.

"Give me that."

"Not till we're done," he teased.

"We are done." She glared at him.

He let out a subtle laugh. "Come on, Bec. We were having a good time."

"Yeah, we *were*." She held out her hand.

He hesitated, but gave her the phone.

The display lit up: one new text message. Becky Lee opened it and read.

"What's it say?" Jesse asked.

"She says she'll wait, but only for a little while."

"Of course she'll wait. She always does."

Becky Lee sighed. He was right. Faithful Sarah waited for her all the time. It wasn't fair. "I want to go back now."

Jesse moved in close. "But we have something to celebrate."

"What? Your big music opportunity?"

"No, silly. Your birthday." He kissed her lips.

She shuddered with desire. "Not till tomorrow."

"It's almost tomorrow," he whispered. Jesse kissed her forehead, then walked to the door and closed it. He turned back to her, smiled, and turned out the light.

Her conscience tugged at her. She really should go back to the party. But she wanted to stay here with Jesse. Sarah had said she'd wait. And tomorrow, when Becky Lee told her all the romantic details about how she and Jesse had rekindled their relationship, her friend would understand.

❦ ❦ ❦

Becky Lee checked her cell-phone messages as Jesse started the car. More than three hours had passed. "Sarah is going to be so mad at me."

She had two text messages and several missed calls. She scrolled through the missed calls. The same phone number appeared six times from one-thirty until three o'clock. She didn't recognize the number, and whoever it was hadn't left a voice-mail message.

The text messages were from Sarah. The first one came in at twelve twenty. *Where r u?*

The second one came in at twelve forty-five. *Leaving now. I'll call tomorrow. Maybe.*

Becky Lee's heart sank. "She went home a couple of hours ago."

Jesse rested his arm on the back of the seat and rubbed Becky Lee's neck. "Guess there wasn't any rush, then."

"I shouldn't have ditched her like that."

Jesse pulled into Becky Lee's driveway. "I'm sure she'll be happy to know we're back together." A sarcastic sparkle gleamed in his eyes from the moonlight shining through the windshield.

Jesse stopped the truck in front of the garage where Denise usually parked. "Looks like your sister's not here."

Becky Lee pulled the handle on the door. "She must have decided to stay at Derek's tonight."

"Can I come in, then?"

"No," Becky Lee said, appalled. "If she came home while you were here, I'd be in big trouble."

He leaned over the center console and kissed her. "Happy Birthday, Bec."

"Thanks." She got out of the truck.

"Want me to walk you in?"

"Good night, Jes."

"I'll call you in a couple of hours."

Becky Lee shut the truck door and waved. As Jesse drove off, she walked into the house and headed up the stairs. In her room, she tossed her purse and her cell phone onto the nightstand, changed into sweats, and climbed under the covers.

As tired as she was, sleep evaded her. She stared up at the ceiling, her mind running through the events of the evening. Her heart leapt with excitement as she realized that she and Jesse were really back together. He would be leaving for Nashville soon, but he had offered her the opportunity to go with him.

Would she be able to walk away from her dream of keeping the ranch? Was it even still her dream? Or was it just a faint memory of something she wanted from the past that didn't even exist anymore? There was nothing left of the place anyway except Peg and King. Was she fooling herself to think she could keep it going?

Tomorrow, Becky Lee would ask Sarah what she thought about all this. *If she's still speaking to me after the way I acted tonight.*

First thing in the morning, she'd call Sarah and apologize profusely, then tell her the good news.

Becky Lee's cell phone rang. The number on the screen was the same as the earlier missed calls. She sat up. "Hello?"

"Becky Lee?"

"Yes."

"It's Tad." His voice broke. "I've been trying to reach you for a couple of hours. Where have you been?"

Becky Lee's defenses went up. What was he doing, checking up on her? "I've been out."

Tad let out a sigh. "There's been an accident."

Panic choked Becky Lee. The memory of her parents' car accident rushed in like flood waters.

"I was volunteering at the hospital when the paramedics brought her in."

"Who?" Alarm bells rang in Becky Lee's head.

"Sarah."

Becky Lee went numb.

"I could come pick you up and take you to the hospital," Tad offered.

Words escaped her.

"Do you want me to come over?"

"Yes. Please."

"I'll be there in a half hour."

Becky dropped the phone on her bed. She sat in shock for several minutes. What could have happened? Did Sarah get drunk at the party and try to drive home on her own? Surely she wouldn't do that. Sarah was smart.

Maybe Danny had driven her home drunk. Or maybe they were both sober but got hit by a drunk driver.

Perhaps alcohol had nothing to do with the accident. Her parents' car accident hadn't been alcohol related.

Becky Lee shook off her second-guessing and slipped on socks and tennis shoes. She hurried downstairs. She'd have to leave Denise a note in case she came home before Becky Lee got back.

When she reached the kitchen cabinet where they kept the notepads, she saw that there was already a sheet of paper on the counter. Denise had written her a note, saying she was staying with Derek that night and would be back by ten the next morning.

A knock sounded on the back door. Becky Lee opened it and Tad stepped in. His eyes were red. Could he have been crying, or was he just tired?

"You okay?" he asked.

She nodded, choking back tears.

"Ready to go?" Tad held out his hand to her.

She stared at it. "No." She wasn't ready. She couldn't face her friend. Not after deserting her.

Tad put his arm around Becky Lee and walked her to the car.

Chapter Seven

ecky Lee sat in the corner of the hospital waiting room. She leaned her head against the wall, drew her knees to her chest, and wrapped her arms around them. Tad sat in a chair beside her. Sarah's parents paced in the hallway in front of the door. A tense silence hung in the air as everyone waited for a doctor or nurse to tell them the outcome of the already four-hour surgery.

Becky Lee closed her eyes, wishing she could shut out the world.

In her mind's eye, she imagined herself with Sarah at the local swimming hole. Sarah stood on the embankment in shorts and a tank top, a rope swing in her hand. She looked nervous, but she was smiling. Becky Lee encouraged her to jump. Sarah finally did. She swung over the water, her thick blonde hair blowing behind her. She let go in the middle and splashed into the pool. A moment later, she came back up, sputtering and laughing.

Becky Lee clapped. "You did it!"

"That was great!" Sarah said, treading out of the water.

"I told you you'd love it."

"You always push me to do things," Sarah said as she pulled herself out of the pond. "If it weren't for you, I'd never have any fun." She hugged Becky Lee, getting her dry clothes all wet, and ran back up the embankment. "I'm going again."

Sarah had always been somewhat timid. Becky Lee liked convincing her friend to try things she wouldn't normally do on her own.

Sarah stood at the top of the embankment, ready to swing again. "Watch this." She leapt into the air and grabbed the rope. It carried her across the beach and over the hole. Only this time it wasn't a pond. It was just a great big empty hole in the ground.

Paralyzing fear struck Becky Lee. "Sarah, don't let go!"

But she did. Sarah fell in.

"Sarah!"

"Becky Lee."

Startled, she slammed her feet to the floor and sat straight up. A police officer stood in front of her. She shot her eyes around the hospital waiting room. Sarah's parents stood behind the officer.

Tad still sat beside her. He touched her shoulder. "Are you all right?"

Her frenetic breathing slowed. She nodded.

The officer, an older man with a mixture of gray and black hair, stepped closer. His eyes looked tired, and the lines in his forehead deepened. "I'm Officer Trenton. I'd like to ask you some questions."

"O-Okay." She scooted back in the seat.

He moved a chair up to her and pulled out a small writing pad and pen from his shirt pocket. "You were at Zack Keiser's party last night, right?"

"Yes."

"Who did you go with?"

"Sarah."

"How long were you there?"

She felt Tad's eyes pierce through her. "An hour or two. I don't really remember."

Officer Trenton wrote on the pad, then looked back at her. "Did you leave with anyone?"

Guilt strangled her breathing. "Y-Yes. My boyfriend. Jesse McCoy."

"Was Sarah still at the party when you left?"

Her throat tightened. She bit her lower lip and nodded.

"Do you know if Sarah had been drinking?"

Becky Lee leaned on the armrest and buried her face in her hand. She let out a muffled "Yes."

"Several people at the party said she became upset and started drinking heavily after her friend left. I presume that friend is you."

This wasn't happening. Sarah never drank very much. She was the one who always drove Becky Lee home after parties.

Officer Trenton flipped back a few pages in his notepad. "I spoke with a young man named Danny McCoy. He talked with Sarah around twelve forty-five. He said she was drunk and very angry. He offered her a ride home, but she left before he got his jacket and keys."

Becky Lee trembled. "Do you know what happened to her?"

Officer Trenton rested his forearms on his legs. "Her car hit a tree two miles from the party," he said, his voice calm. "Preliminary reports indicate she was doing almost seventy when she hit it."

Becky Lee broke into sobs. "I should have gone back for her. If she dies, it's my fault."

Sarah's mom knelt in front of Becky Lee and took her hands. Her face streamed with tears. "Sarah's going to be fine, honey. You'll see." She pulled Becky Lee close and hugged her. "She'll be okay."

Becky Lee wished she could believe that.

❧ ❧ ❧

Another hour and a half passed with no word from the doctor about Sarah. Becky Lee still sat in the same chair. Tad was standing, looking out the window. Sarah's dad slumped in a chair, her mom sleeping next to him with her head on his shoulder.

The waiting room door opened. A doctor, wearing blue scrubs, entered, his face looking tired. Becky Lee jumped to her feet as did Sarah's parents. Tad came up beside her.

The doctor took off his surgeon's cap and extended a hand. "Mr. and Mrs. Moretti, I'm Dr. Salvatore."

Sarah's dad shook his hand. "How is my Sarah?"

"Won't you please sit down," the doctor said in a low voice.

God, no. Don't take Sarah from us.

Sarah's mom looked at her husband, fear in her eyes. He eased her into a chair, then sat next to her.

Becky Lee swallowed hard. Tad took her hand.

"Is she going to be all right?" Sarah's mom asked.

The doctor hesitated. "There was internal bleeding."

Becky Lee stopped breathing. Tad squeezed her hand.

"There was also severe brain damage. I'm sorry. There was nothing we could do."

Becky Lee crumpled to the floor as realization dawned. "No!"

Chapter Eight

Becky Lee turned Denise's truck off the main road onto the gravel lane that led to her house. She parked in front of the garage and turned off the engine. She had left in the middle of Sarah's funeral without telling anyone. She needed to be alone.

As she stepped out of the vehicle, she realized that the last time Sarah was there, they were getting ready for that stupid party.

What am I going to do without her?

She shuffled up the path to the porch, unlocked the front door, and ran up the stairs. She slammed her door and threw herself onto her bed. *I can't believe she's dead. And it's all my fault.* She buried her face in her pillow and cried for several minutes.

A soft knock sounded on her door. Denise entered. "You okay?"

Becky Lee wiped her eyes and stared at the ceiling. "Is the funeral over already?"

Denise sat on the edge of the bed. "I saw you leave, so I asked Derek to take home. I didn't think you should be alone right now."

"I left Sarah alone," she said sharply.

"You can't blame yourself."

"Yeah, I can."

"You weren't driving the car."

"I might as well have been."

Denise pulled on an exposed thread on the comforter.

Jenn A. Sesto

"You know I'm right," Becky Lee said. "That's why you're not saying anything."

"Okay. If you'd gone back to the party, maybe the accident wouldn't have happened. But Sarah got into the car of her own free will."

Becky Lee sat up, her jaw tight. "She was mad at me. And she was drunk. I only had one beer before I left. I could have driven her home if I'd gone back."

Denise pushed Becky Lee's hair behind her ear and caressed her cheek. "I'm so sorry, sweetie. I wish I could somehow fix this for you."

"Well, you can't."

Denise held out her arms. "Come here."

Becky Lee scooted closer.

Denise hugged her. "Don't beat yourself up. It's not going to bring her back."

"I know."

Denise held her for a long moment. "Do you think Jesse will come over after the funeral is over?"

"No. I told him I wanted to be alone today. Why?"

"Tad called earlier. He wanted to know if he could come over this evening."

Becky Lee rolled her eyes and moaned. "No."

"Why?"

"I don't want him judging me."

"He wouldn't do that. He's a friend who's concerned about you."

"I don't want to see him."

Denise stood. "I'm going to make lunch for Derek. Do you want something?"

"No. I'm too tired."

"Okay." Denise nodded and left the room, shutting the door behind her.

❧ ❧ ❧

Becky Lee awoke after a couple of hours of fitful sleep. She rubbed her eyes, got up, and moped down the hall to the stairs.

As she descended the steps, she heard voices. Derek, Denise, and Tad. What was Tad doing there? Denise probably hadn't told him not to come over, like Becky Lee had asked her to.

As she reached the bottom stair, she heard Tad ask, "Why don't you all come to church with me on Sunday?"

"That's a good idea," Derek said. "I've been wanting to go back to church for a long time now. What do you think, Denise?"

"I don't know." Her voice had a nervous tone. "What about Becky Lee? She won't want to go."

"She might," Derek replied.

"Let's ask her," Tad said.

Becky Lee entered the kitchen and looked at the three sitting around the table, empty coffee cups in front of them. "I don't want to go to church."

Disappointment flashed across Tad's face. "Will you at least think about it?" he asked quietly.

She went to the fridge, opened it, and stared at the contents. "What's there to eat?" She glanced back at Denise.

"We were talking about getting some pizza in town," she said. "Do you want to come?"

"No. I'll find something here."

"Is there someplace else you'd like to go?" Denise asked.

Becky Lee didn't have the energy to make anything. Or to argue. "Actually, pizza's fine."

❧ ❧ ❧

"It's kind of crowded for a Tuesday night," Becky Lee said as they walked through the pizza parlor door. Only two tables remained vacant. All the

Jenn A. Sesto

arcade games had players. She recognized some of the kids from school. She hoped they wouldn't hound her about Sarah's accident.

"Would you prefer to order the pizza and take it back home to eat?" Denise suggested.

"Sounds good to me," Derek said.

"Me too," Tad added.

Becky Lee sat at a table near the counter. Denise placed their order, then they all joined her. While they waited, they engaged in casual conversation, but Becky Lee didn't really listen to anything they were saying.

Within twenty minutes they were back in the car, the aromas of pepperoni, sausage, and mushrooms filling the air.

From the front seat, Denise turned back to Becky Lee. "I know you're hungry. Go ahead and have a piece now if you'd like."

"Actually, the smell of the pizza is making me nauseous." Becky Lee leaned back on the head rest. She felt like she could sleep for days.

Chapter Nine

The sun shone through the partially open blinds onto Becky Lee's face as she lay on the bed. For the first time in a week, she wanted to get up. She'd taken several days off from school and slept through most of it. Every time she got up, she felt sick. Today, she felt hungry. A big improvement.

She took a long shower. When she got out, she smelled bacon cooking. That made her stomach rumble. She dressed quickly and headed downstairs. Denise stood at the stove, stirring scrambled eggs. Toast popped up from the toaster.

"What are you doing up?" Becky Lee asked. Denise never rose early on Sunday mornings.

Denise turned to Becky Lee, spatula in hand. "I heard you get in the shower, so I thought I'd make a nice breakfast for us. I hope you're hungry."

"Yeah, finally."

"It's ready, so have a seat." Denise piled scrambled eggs, a couple of pieces of bacon, and a slice of toast on a plate and set it on the table in front of Becky Lee.

"I may not be able to finish all that."

Denise filled another plate. "Eat what you can. Coffee is ready if you want."

"This is fine." Becky Lee grabbed the orange juice pitcher and a glass from the center of the table. She poured the juice and took a sip.

Denise sat across from Becky Lee with her plate. "I was getting worried about you, not eating anything all week."

Becky Lee chomped on a piece of bacon. "I've been too tired to eat."

"That happens when your emotions get out of whack." Denise poured herself a glass of juice.

"Well, I'm feeling a lot better now." Becky Lee gobbled down several forkfuls of the eggs, savoring their flavor. Getting her appetite back made her feel so hungry she thought she could eat a whole chicken and maybe a whole pig too. "So, why are you really up so early?"

Denise's sheepish look told Becky Lee there was another motive.

"I know you didn't do all this just for me."

"I did it because I wanted to." She took a bite of her toast. "But I'm also going into the city to meet Derek and Tad."

Becky Lee frowned. "For church?"

Denise's eyes probed Becky Lee's. "Yes. We'd all like it if you'd come."

"No way."

"Why not?"

"If church was so important, why didn't Mom and Daddy take us? They never even mentioned God's name except when they were mad."

Denise sighed. "Tad and I have been talking a lot lately. He's been praying for us."

"We don't need his sympathy." Anger rose in Becky Lee. "He wasn't here when our parents died. We handled that just fine. And he can't bring Sarah back. So I don't see how praying and going to church will help now."

"I really want to know about God. And Derek wants to get back into church too. He hasn't been since junior high."

"Well, good for you. Do what you want." Becky Lee dropped her last piece of bacon back on her plate. Her stomach knotted up. She wondered if she was getting sick again or if this topic of conversation was making her feel ill.

Truth to tell, part of her wanted to go to church. But the people there would judge her, of that she was certain. She did things they wouldn't approve of. And she wasn't going to change.

"I'd love it if you'd come, at least once."

Becky Lee sighed. Knowing her sister would not drop this until she agreed, she shrugged.

"Wonderful!" Denise's face beamed. "You should wear something nice, not jeans. But not one of your party dresses either."

"Great. Now I have to worry about how I dress?"

Denise smiled and took a bite of scrambled eggs.

Becky Lee's stomach tightened more. She stood.

"Aren't you going to finish eating?" Denise asked.

"My stomach's upset."

"Probably too much for it too handle after being empty all week. Be ready to leave for church by nine, okay?"

Becky Lee trudged back up to her room.

Staring into her closet, she saw only three dresses hung up. Her party dresses, as Denise called them. On the floor lay the dress she'd worn in the last family portrait. She hadn't wanted to wear it after her parents died. But it seemed the only thing suitable for church.

Becky Lee put on the dress and looked at herself in the long mirror hanging on the back of her door. "Yeah, I guess this looks okay."

As she zipped up the back, a wave of nausea hit her. She cursed herself for eating as she ran to the bathroom.

A few minutes later, Becky Lee returned to her room and sat on her bed. She felt better. But maybe she shouldn't go to church if she had something contagious, like the flu.

Denise had been so excited when she said she'd go. Becky Lee didn't want to tell her no now. Besides, she was starting to feel kind of enthusiastic about it herself.

She chalked up her upset stomach to emotional stress and eating too much on an empty stomach, like Denise said. If she didn't eat anything else until she got back home, she should be fine.

Jenn A. Sesto

❦ ❦ ❦

Denise didn't say much as she drove into the city. She seemed deep in thought. Becky Lee was okay with not talking. Staying still and quiet kept her stomach from being agitated.

When Denise reached Oak Street, she turned and drove another block. She pulled into a gravel parking lot. Most of the spaces had already been taken, so she parked at the far end.

She turned off the ignition and turned to Becky Lee. "You ready for this?"

Becky Lee chuckled. "How do you get ready to go into a church?"

Denise sighed. "Okay, here we go."

Becky Lee opened her door and slipped out of the truck. As soon as her feet touched the ground, a wave of nausea overcame her. Light-headedness accompanied it. She drew in a deep breath, and it subsided.

"Come on. We'll be late." Denise stared up at the church.

Becky Lee shut her door. Once she sat down, she was sure she'd be fine.

As she and Denise walked across the parking lot, Becky Lee stared at the two-story building. The roofline peaked in the center and the sides angled down, giving it an A-frame look. Multicolored stained-glass windows ran the length of the nearest side of the building. A large cross stood on the awning above the entrance.

Two large wooden doors opened outward. A line of people walked up to the doors, where an older man in a dark blue suit and an equally old woman in a floral dress greeted them, shook their hands, and gave each of them a folded piece of paper.

Denise shot Becky Lee an uneasy look, then they proceeded to the doors.

The woman extended her hand to Becky Lee. Her pretty pink nail polish matched her toenails, which showed through her open-toed sandals.

78

Shaking Becky Lee's hand, the woman said, "Welcome." She held out the folded paper. "Here's a program."

Becky Lee took it and stepped into the foyer, her sister following.

"There they are," Denise said.

Becky Lee followed her to Tad and Derek, who stood by a table with brochures and books on it.

"Hey, you two," Derek said when the girls approached.

Tad looked up from the book he was examining and smiled. "You decided to come." He gave Becky Lee a hug.

She tensed. Surely he would get in trouble for hugging her in front of everyone.

"Relax," Tad said into her ear. Pulling back, he turned to Denise and Derek. "Let's get a seat."

Tad took Becky Lee's hand. She tried to pull back, but he tightened his grip and led her into the sanctuary. He introduced her and Denise and Derek to several people as they moved down the aisle of pews. To Becky Lee's surprise, everyone welcomed them warmly.

"How about here?" Tad stopped at the fourth pew from the front.

Denise glanced at the stage, then back at Tad. "So close?"

Derek chuckled. "What difference does it make?" He slid into the pew and sat down.

Denise sat beside Derek. Tad motioned Becky Lee in next, then sat beside her.

Becky Lee looked around the church. Wooden planks covered the ceiling, extending from the peaked roofline down to the stained-glass windows on both sides of the church. Three rows of pews extended from the stage to the sanctuary entrance. Each row had twenty-five or thirty pews. Most of them were filled, so people started filling in the open spaces around where they sat.

She opened her program and read the announcement page. Youth group meetings were offered, as well as adult Bible studies. Other services included mentorship classes, premarital and marriage counseling, and pregnancy support groups. The list went on, but when the room grew quiet, Becky Lee looked up.

Two men and three women walked up the steps onto the stage. Except for one of the women, they each grabbed a microphone from the music stands lined up behind the podium. The other woman sat at the piano, which was off to the side, and began playing.

The audience stood and sang. Not knowing the lyrics, Becky Lee watched those around her. Some people had their eyes closed while they sang, others raised their arms into the air. Becky Lee turned to Tad and saw that he was doing both.

After the song ended, one of the men told everyone to have a seat. As the attendees sat, the singers and the pianist walked off the stage and sat as well.

A man in a dark brown suit went up to the podium and asked everyone to bow their heads. Becky Lee did, but she felt self-conscious about it. Thinking people might be watching her, she glanced up, but everyone's head was bowed. Feeling foolish, she lowered hers back down.

When the prayer ended, a few people from the front rows stood, each holding a round tray. Starting at the front rows, they handed the tray to the person on the end of the pew. Each person passed the tray along until it ended up at the opposite end. Everyone placed something into the tray, but she couldn't tell what.

She leaned into Tad. "What are those?"

"Offering plates." He held a twenty-dollar bill in his hand. "You put donations in them."

Becky Lee turned to her sister. "Do we—"

"Derek's got it," Denise whispered.

Derek dropped a check into the tray and passed it to Denise. She handed it over Becky Lee's lap to Tad. Tad dropped in his twenty and gave the tray to the man waiting at the end of the pew. Becky Lee watched until all the offering plates had been collected and the collectors left the sanctuary. She wondered what they were going to do with the money.

The man in the dark brown suit opened a thick book and laid it on the podium. He said another prayer, a shorter one this time. He read from the book, then paced across the stage, speaking to the audience.

Becky Lee didn't really understand what he was talking about. It seemed like gibberish, or some foreign language. She felt ridiculous sitting there when nothing made sense. She shifted in the hard seat and sighed.

Denise nudged her arm and shot her a warning look.

She sank into her seat and mouthed, "Sorry."

Tad bumped her. She looked up at him. He winked.

She grinned uneasily, then forced her attention back to the pastor. She tried harder to understand what he was talking about.

The man read from the book, "The righteous cry out, and the Lord hears, and delivers them out of all their troubles. The Lord is near to those who have a broken heart."

She'd had a broken heart ever since Sarah's death. Did that mean the Lord was near her?

The pastor continued reading, "Trust in the Lord with all your heart, and lean not on your own understanding. In all your ways acknowledge Him, and He shall direct your paths."

Becky Lee didn't trust anything she couldn't see with her own eyes or put her hands on. She glanced around the room. People seemed to be absorbing every word. What were they thinking?

When the man finished his talk, the pianist returned to the stage and played. The audience stood and sang again. After the pastor said another short prayer, everyone stood to leave.

Becky Lee hung back as Denise and her boyfriend walked toward the exit, Tad talking to them about the sermon. She sang in her mind a few words that stuck in her head from the last song.

At the truck, Becky Lee reached for the door handle. A wave of nausea stopped her. She drew in a deep breath, then let it out slowly. She needed to sit down.

She pulled on the handle. The door was locked.

A loud whooshing sound crashed in her head like a tidal wave. She saw spots. Her surroundings became foggy.

"D-Denise."

She barely saw her sister turn around on the other side the truck.

Denise's eyes widened.

Becky Lee collapsed.

❦ ❦ ❦

Becky Lee woke up with a feeling of confusion. She opened her eyes, but her lids felt heavy. When her blurry vision finally cleared, she realized she was lying in a hospital bed. *What am I doing here?*

The sound of a machine kicking on caught her attention. Something squeezed her arm. The blood-pressure cuff grew tighter until she almost couldn't stand it anymore. Then it slowly deflated. The machine beeped as the green number on the black screen changed from 160 to 158...156...154, until it stopped at 132. Then another number displayed. It started at 112 and dropped to 82. A narrow strip of paper fed through the machine as data printed on it.

The door opened. A gray-haired man in a long white coat and a stethoscope around his neck entered, Denise close behind him.

"You're awake." Relief filled Denise's voice.

"Hello, Becky Lee. I'm Dr. Ross." He checked the blood-pressure machine, then turned to her. "How are you feeling?"

"Exhausted."

The doctor picked up her arm and placed his finger on the inside of her wrist. He studied his watch for several seconds, then rested her arm back on the bed. "You gave your sister quite a scare."

The memory of standing beside the truck after church rushed back to her. "I was dizzy."

Dr. Ross pulled out a small flashlight from a coat pocket. He flashed the light in her eyes. "Denise tells me you've had quite a week. I'm sorry about your friend." He smiled gently. "When was the last time you ate anything?"

"This morning. I haven't felt like eating much lately. But when I woke up, I was starving."

"What did you have?"

"Bacon, scrambled eggs, toast, orange juice."

The doctor nodded thoughtfully. He moved to the other side of the bed and rolled up Becky Lee's sleeve.

Seeing a small plastic tube stuck in her arm with tape over it, she let out a gasp. "What's that?"

"I'm going to hook you up to this IV." Dr. Ross unraveled a tube that was coiled around a hook on a metal stand. "You're a little undernourished. And your initial blood work shows some dehydration. This will help with both. I'd like you to stay here for a few hours so we can monitor you."

Becky Lee rolled her eyes. "Do I have a choice?"

"No," Denise piped in.

"In the meantime," the doctor continued, "I'm going to have the lab run a few more tests, just to be sure."

A twinge of fear struck Becky Lee. "Be sure of what?"

"That nothing else is going on. It shouldn't take long."

"Thank you, Doctor." Denise walked with him to the door.

"Her other friends can come in now," he said, leaving the room.

Denise returned to Becky Lee and caressed the back of her hand. "You okay?"

"Yeah. Just tired." She narrowed her eyes. "This is crazy. All I've done all week is sleep."

"Sometimes getting too much sleep makes me more tired."

"I guess."

Denise tucked in her blankets. "I'm going to go let the guys know how you're doing."

Becky Lee lifted her head. "What guys?"

"Derek and Tad."

"Tad's here?"

Denise nodded.

"Don't let him come in. I don't want to see him." She couldn't stand the thought of him feeling sorry for her.

A slow smile worked its way into Denise's eyes. "You know, Tad was pretty worried about you when you collapsed."

"So what? He's my friend."

Denise grinned. "It seems to me his feelings for you go beyond friendship."

"You don't say," she said, pretending disinterest.

Denise's eyes sparkled. "When you fell, Tad was the first one around the truck. He laid you on the tailgate and told Derek to call 911, although Derek was already on the phone. He put his coat under your head, and…"

Denise sounded like a junior high school girl telling her that the cutest guy in class liked her. Becky Lee chuckled inside. It had been a long time since she'd seen Denise act so giddy. But what her sister said didn't surprise her. Tad would have helped anyone in the same way.

"You should have seen his face while we waited for the ambulance. There was actual fear in his eyes. I think they even teared up. He caressed your face and talked to you, told you everything was going to be okay."

Becky Lee stared at the ceiling. Could Denise be right? She shook her head. She could not allow herself to believe Tad liked her as anything more than a friend.

"You don't look like you're interested in hearing this." Denise sounded disappointed.

Becky Lee shifted her gaze to her sister. "Tad was just being a good friend."

"Believe what you want," she teased. "But you didn't see his face." She kissed Becky Lee on the forehead. Her expression more serious, she said, "I'll let the nurses know we'll be in the cafeteria. Have them page me if you need anything."

Becky Lee grinned. "I'm sure I won't need anything."

Denise exited the room, letting the door close behind her.

A sense of hope leaped in her heart. What would it mean if Tad did like her as more than just a friend? She thought about it until her brain hurt. Finally, her eyes drifted shut and she let sleep take over.

❦ ❦ ❦

Becky Lee heard Dr. Ross's voice in the hallway. It was about time. She was going stir crazy waiting. She sat up, propped her pillow against the wall, and leaned back on it.

Dr. Ross entered the room, smiling, but his eyes had a concerned look in them.

"Is everything okay?" she asked.

"Yes. And no." He pulled up a chair and sat down.

Panic gripped her.

"Becky Lee, I'm not sure how to tell you this, but…you're pregnant."

Chapter Ten

*B*ecky Lee's doctor released her from the hospital, giving her medication for nausea. She slept for most of the next two days, not wanting to accept the grim news of her reality.

Jesse called her cell phone so often Sunday afternoon and Monday, she turned it off. Monday evening he called the house several times, though Denise repeatedly told him Becky Lee was sick and would call when she felt better.

As Denise headed for bed Monday night, she told Becky Lee, "You're going to have to face Jesse sooner or later."

"I know," she groaned.

The next morning, after dialing and hanging up three times, Becky Lee sent Jesse a text message, asking him to meet her at her house after school. He had responded that he would ...and that he couldn't wait to get her answer on Nashville.

She grabbed her sweatshirt off the chair and slipped it over her head. Then she went out the front door and sat in the porch swing. She closed her eyes and rested her head on the cushion as she swung.

What would she say to Jesse? Their lives were about to change, but not in the way he expected.

How could she take care of a baby? Babies cried, always needed to be held, had diapers that had to be changed, were up all night long. She breathed a heavy sigh. No more parties. No more doing what she wanted to do when she wanted to do it.

And what about Jesse? Would he help? Her heart told her he would. A baby would bring them together once and for all. But her head said no. He would not be there for her or the baby. He had his own plans for the future.

Hearing footsteps on the gravel, she lifted her head and opened her eyes. Jesse strolled up the driveway. She felt a strong urge to run down the steps and throw herself into his arms, but she remained seated until he came up the steps. His beautiful brown eyes sparkled. His eager smile invited her into his open arms. When she hesitated, his eyes narrowed.

Becky Lee's throat tightened. Tears rimmed her eyes. It was over between them. The feeling rushed in like floodwaters.

The lines between Jesse's eyes deepened. He knelt in front her, taking her hand in his. "Bec, what's wrong?"

Her lips trembled as she searched for the right words. When they didn't come, she shook her head. "I-I can't....."

"Can't what?"

She stared deep into his eyes. He would be leaving in a couple of days, and this was the last time she'd be with him, her last opportunity to touch him. She ran her fingers through his soft hair and cupped his face in her palms. She kissed him softly, letting her lips linger on his, savoring the warmth and feel of the last time.

Pulling away, she whispered, "I love you, Jes." Her voice broke. She swallowed hard. "But I can't go with you to Nashville."

A hint of fear clouded his eyes. "Why?"

"I just can't. But you need to go. Chase your dream."

"I want you to come with me."

She shook her head. Tears welled up in her eyes. "It won't work."

"Yeah, it will. I know I've been a jerk in the past, but I'll change. I promise."

"No. It has to be over."

Jesse leaped back. "But why? You have to give me a reason."

"It's just a feeling."

"You're breaking up with me over a feeling? You won't even give this a chance?"

"No," she said softly but firmly.

Jesse squeezed his eyes with his hand. He took a deep breath and looked back at her. "Think about it for a while longer," he said, his voice desperate. "You said you wanted to finish school. You could join me after graduation."

"I won't be coming, Jesse. I'm sorry."

He took a step back and bumped into the chair along the railing. He turned, picked it up, and threw it against the side of the house.

Becky Lee jumped. Fear filled her. Would he hurt her?

Fury flashed across his face. His jaw muscle popped in and out. "Okay. Fine. If this is what you want."

"I-It is."

A truck pulled up the driveway and stopped at the garage. Denise jumped out, her eyes questioning Becky Lee.

Jesse glanced at Denise, then back at Becky Lee. "Is she the reason you decided this?"

"No. I never even told her about Nashville."

He threw his hands in the air. "Whatever. Have a nice life."

Becky Lee bit her lip as she watched Jesse leap off the porch, missing all the steps. He brushed past Denise on the path without even acknowledging her and stormed down the long driveway to the road.

Denise rushed up the steps. Her eyes moved from Becky Lee to the chair leaning on its side against the house, then back to Becky Lee. "Are you all right?"

She drew in a deep breath. "Yeah."

"Did you tell him?"

She stared into the distance, realizing that she had sent Jesse out of her life for good. "No."

Denise's eyebrows raised. "You didn't?"

Becky Lee covered her face with her hands. "I couldn't."

Denise sat beside her and put an arm around her. "Then why was he so mad?"

Becky Lee watched Jesse traipsing down the road toward his house next door. "He's leaving for Nashville this week. He wanted me to go, but I told him no."

"Nashville? When did this come up?"

"He told me the night before my birthday." She swallowed hard. "Some agent or producer or something asked him to bring a demo tape."

Denise's face twisted. "What does that have to do with not telling him you're pregnant?"

Becky Lee stood and looked out over the edge of the porch. Jesse turned up his driveway and disappeared into the house. "He's moving on with his life. It's over between us."

Denise sprang up and moved in front of Becky Lee. "He has a responsibility to you. You have to tell him."

Becky Lee glared at her sister. "No, I don't. And you won't either. I want him to leave without knowing." Denise opened her mouth to speak, but Becky Lee cut her off. "He will never know. All right?"

Denise took a step back. "What do you think you're going to do? Raise this baby by yourself?"

Tears filled her eyes. "I don't know what I'm going to do." She collapsed into sobs.

"Come here, sweetie." Denise wrapped her arms around Becky Lee and held her tight. "I don't know if you're making the right choice, but we'll handle this together. Okay?"

She pulled back. "Thank you."

Denise brushed Becky Lee's hair behind her ear and wiped the tears from her cheeks. "I'd like you to talk with someone at the church about your options. They have counseling—"

"Absolutely not. The church isn't going to tell me what to do. It's my life and my choice."

"What about talking to Tad?"

"He's the last person I want to talk to about this." Tad was such a good person, so godly. With all her drinking, premarital sex, and now being pregnant and not married, she was hardly the kind of Christian girl he'd go for. And she never would be.

"You have to talk to somebody, Bec."

"Not if I decide to have an abortion."

Denise's eyes widened. "You wouldn't."

Becky Lee's throat felt tight. "I might." She stood and turned to the door.

Denise grabbed her arm and spun her around. "I won't let you."

"You can't stop me."

Chapter Eleven

ecky Lee waited until Denise left for work before leaving her bedroom. She had decided to skip school that day and try to get an appointment at an abortion clinic.

She hurried down to the kitchen and pulled the phone book out of a drawer. She looked up the number for the nearest clinic. With trembling hands, she dialed.

The phone rang about ten times before a woman answered. Suddenly, Becky Lee didn't know what to say.

"Hello? Is anyone there?"

"Yeah. I-I'm here."

"How can I help you?"

Her legs weakened. She sat in a chair at the kitchen table. "I need to make an appointment."

"Have you been here before?"

"No."

"Okay. What do you need an appointment for?"

Becky Lee's voice quivered. "I …um …I need to have an abortion."

"Do you know how far along you are in your pregnancy?"

"I just found out. I guess a couple of weeks."

"When was your last menstrual period?"

"I don't know. Maybe a couple of months ago."

"We'll do a sonogram to determine exactly how far along you are.

Hold on just a moment." Becky Lee heard typing on a keyboard. "We had a cancellation this morning, so I have an opening in a half hour. Can you come in then?"

"Yeah. I'll be there."

Becky Lee ran upstairs, deciding to skip her morning shower. As she dressed, her stomach lurched with nausea. Breathing steadily and moving slowly, she splashed cool water on her face, blotted it with a towel, and pulled a brush through her hair. Then she went back downstairs and found some saltine crackers, which she nibbled on between small sips of water.

Soon she'd be able to eat again without getting sick. That would be great. She hoped she could get the procedure scheduled quickly. She was sick and tired of feeling sick and tired.

Looking at the clock, she realized she needed to leave. She took the last bite of cracker and another sip of water, then grabbed her purse, eager to get this over with.

❧ ❧ ❧

Becky Lee arrived at the clinic five minutes early. Turned out to be a good thing, because the receptionist made her fill out a lot of paperwork. When she got to the question that asked who the father was, she panicked. If she put Jesse's name on the form, would someone call him and tell him about the pregnancy? She left the line blank.

Just as she finished the paperwork and turned it in to the woman at the front desk, a lady came out into the waiting room and called Becky Lee's name. She led her down a hallway into a small room. She handed her a gown and told her to change into it. "A technician will be in soon."

Dressed in the thin cloth gown, with the opening in the front as requested, Becky Lee sat on the narrow bed, her bare feet dangling over the edge.

A technician came in with a clipboard. "Hi, I'm Maria. I'll be doing your sonogram today." She read the form Becky Lee had filled out. "So, you don't know when your last period was?"

"I don't remember having one last month."

"Okay. Go ahead and lie back."

Trying to stop shaking, Becky Lee did as she was instructed.

Maria opened a drawer and pulled out a small tube and something that looked like a large electric razor, but with a wider tip. "I'm going to put some jelly on your abdomen. Then I'll run this transducer over your belly so we can get some measurements."

Maria rolled a machine with a computer monitor on it close to the bed. She flipped several switches and lights flickered. The monitor went black except for some text at the bottom of the screen that was too small for Becky Lee to read. Maria punched keys on the keyboard, watching the monitor as she typed.

Maria smiled, opened the thin gown enough to expose Becky Lee's stomach, and squirted jelly over it. To Becky Lee's surprise it felt warm.

Maria placed the transducer over Becky Lee's navel and moved it slowly. The wand felt soft as it glided over her skin.

After studying the screen for several moments with an intent look, Maria's face relaxed. "There we go." She typed with her left hand while she continued to move the transducer.

Becky Lee wondered what she was seeing.

Within ten minutes or so, Maria turned to Becky Lee. "Okay, all done."

"What were you doing?"

Maria wiped the jelly off Becky Lee's tummy with a towel. "Measuring the baby."

"You could see the baby?" Becky Lee closed her gown and sat up. "Can I see it?"

"No." Maria turned off the machine. "Seeing the baby or hearing the heartbeat may—"

"You can hear the heartbeat?" A strange surge of excitement ran through her.

Maria glanced over her shoulder at the closed door, then lowered her voice. "I'm not supposed to let patients see the monitor or hear the heart-beat."

"But I really want to." Becky Lee hadn't expected to feel so strongly about this, but she did.

"If you do, you may struggle with your decision to have an abortion."

"I doubt that," Becky Lee said.

The technician chewed on her lower lip. "All right. Lie back down."

Becky Lee did as she was instructed.

Maria turned the monitor so Becky Lee could see it. She squirted more jelly on her stomach and moved the transducer around again. "Look," she said. With her finger, she outlined a tiny image on the screen.

Becky Lee leaned up a little to look closer. "It's so fuzzy. And kind of jumpy."

"Your baby is pretty active right now."

Becky Lee stopped breathing for a second. The baby was moving around inside her?

"Here's the head." Maria circled her finger on the screen. "And the body ...and legs."

"That's my baby?" Becky Lee's eyes watered, but she didn't feel sad. She actually felt happy.

Maria pressed a button on the machine. The image on the screen became still. "From this angle, you can see the toes." She turned back to Becky Lee. "Do you want to hear the heartbeat?"

"Can I?"

Maria flipped a switch on the machine. A fast-paced whooshing sound came through the speakers.

"I can hear it." Her baby had a heartbeat. It was real.

Maria set the transducer on the machine and wiped Becky Lee's belly clean. "Based on this, I'd say you're about ten weeks along."

Becky Lee did some quick calculation in her head. "That's two and a half months."

Maria nodded. She tore off a strip of paper from the side of the machine, then turned it off. "You can get dressed now. A counselor will be in to talk with you shortly."

"A counselor?"

"Standard procedure." Maria handed her the paper from the machine. "Becky Lee, I want you to have this. But please don't let anyone know I gave it to you. It's strictly against policy. I could lose my job if anyone found out I let you see the monitor and hear the heartbeat." She sighed. "But I've only been working here for a few days, and I don't think I'm going to last much longer anyway."

Becky Lee glanced down at the paper. It was a black-and-white picture of the baby's feet and toes. Her eyes teared up.

Maria stood. "Think hard about your choice. You don't belong here any more than I do." She left the room, closing the door behind her.

Becky Lee felt confused. She stared at the photo. The baby was real. It already had toes …and a heartbeat. Maybe Denise was right. Perhaps aborting this child would be murder. She needed to get out of this place before the counselor came in.

She set her baby's picture on the bed and dressed quickly. Just as she was putting on her shoes, a knock sounded on the door. It opened. Becky Lee sat back on the bed, covering the black-and-white picture with her hand.

A tall woman, with dark brown hair pulled back in a bun, entered the room, holding a chart. She sat in the chair Maria had sat in. "Hi, Becky Lee. I'm Deborah." She extended her hand.

"Hello." Becky Lee shook her hand.

Deborah flipped the chart open. As she read, she pushed tendrils of hair off her forehead and adjusted her glasses. She sighed several times.

Becky Lee slid the picture under her leg.

Deborah looked up from the chart. "You didn't write down the father's name," she said, her tone matter-of-fact. "Is that because you don't know who the father is?"

Becky Lee swallowed hard. What kind of person did this woman think she was? "I don't want the father to know about this."

"You can give me a name, or I'll write *unknown*."

The coldness in Deborah's voice made Becky Lee want to cry. "I-I don't know if this is what I want after all. I need to think about it more."

Deborah closed the chart and stood. Her face softened slightly. "I know this is a tough choice. But you need to decide very soon if you want to go through with this. We can't perform an abortion after twelve weeks. You're already ten weeks along. We have an opening late next week. I suggest you take that appointment."

"I understand."

"Here's my card." Deborah pulled a card out of the pocket of her shirt and handed it to Becky Lee. "You can call me if you have any questions or even if you just want to talk. If I'm not available, you can speak to one of the other counselors here. We take calls any time of the day or night."

Becky Lee stared at the card, fighting tears.

"I know you don't want to talk to the father about this, but is there someone else you can talk with?"

Immediately Tad came to mind. She tried to push his soft, gentle eyes and understanding smile out of her mind. "Yes," she said, her voice low.

"Good." Deborah pushed the chair back and stepped toward the door. "It's not our job to persuade you one way or the other. But whatever you choose, it'll be final."

"I know." Becky Lee reached under her leg and touched the picture.

"Please stop at the front desk to schedule your appointment. You can always cancel it." Deborah opened the door. "Good luck with your decision." She left the room, leaving the door open.

Becky Lee pulled the picture out from under her leg and stared at her baby's little toes. There was no way she could do this. She'd be murdering her own baby. She felt a sudden longing to talk to Tad.

She grabbed her purse, holding the picture tight in her hand. She walked down the hall to the waiting room, keeping her eyes on the white tiled floor, careful not to make eye contact with anyone wondering through the hallway. She pushed through the door and passed the front desk as quickly as she could without arousing suspicion. She wanted nothing more to do with the place.

Once she made it out the front door and into the cool air outside, she drew in a long, deep breath.

She had to call Tad. She pulled her cell phone out of her purse and scrolled to his number in her address book. She placed the call and waited anxiously for him to answer.

"Hello."

Her heart skipped a beat.

"Hi, Tad. It's me, Becky Lee."

"Hi, Bec. What's up?"

"Are you busy? Can you come over?"

He hesitated. "Aren't you supposed to be in school?"

"Yes, but I have something important to show you."

"Okay. I'll be there as soon as I can."

Becky Lee closed her phone. She couldn't wait to show Tad her baby.

❦ ❦ ❦

Becky Lee was sitting in the porch swing, holding her baby's picture, when Tad pulled up. His eyes twinkled as he climbed the steps. His grin told her he was curious about what she was up to.

"So, what has you so fired up?"

Becky Lee scooted over in the swing and patted the cushion next to her. "Come here and sit down."

Tad did as she requested. He leaned back and rested his arm along the back.

She held out the picture in front of him.

His grin disappeared and his face twisted with confusion. He looked up at her, his eyes questioning.

"That's my baby." She pointed at the picture. "There's the feet...and toes."

Tad stared at the image for several seconds. "Where did you get this?"

Becky Lee stared at the picture in Tad's gentle hands. "I-I went to an abortion clinic this morning." She looked into his face to gauge his reaction. His blue eyes held hers, soft and intent. Her heart swelled. For a brief moment she wished he was the father of her baby.

"Are you going to go through with it?" he asked, not taking his eyes off her.

"I can't. I'm going to keep my baby."

"Have you told Jesse?"

Becky Lee looked away and shook her head. "No."

"He has a right to know," Tad said, his voice tender.

Becky Lee took the picture out of Tad's hand and traced her baby with her finger. "Maybe someday. But not now." She knew Jesse would try to make her change her mind. Make her see that getting an abortion would be the best thing and then she could move to Nashville and be with him. But it was over between them. She'd made that final.

Tad lifted her chin and caressed her cheek. "I don't want you to feel alone in this."

She locked into his gaze. She didn't understand why he seemed to care so much for her. "I've got my sister." The words came out cracked.

"I'd like to be there for you too. If you'll let me."

Becky Lee's heart raced. She did want him with her. Even if just as her friend. "Thank you."

"I won't let you down, Bec. I promise."

He wasn't the type of person to lie. Her heart told her to trust him. But why would he make such a promise? She had nothing to offer him in return.

Tad sat back in the swing. He reached out for the picture. "May I look at it again?"

She handed it to him.

He gazed at it thoughtfully. "Why would an abortion clinic give you a picture of your baby?"

Becky Lee thought about Maria. "They weren't supposed to. But I had a really nice lady who'd only been there a few days. She let me hear the baby's heartbeat too."

Tad rubbed his chin. "That's really odd." He looked up and handed her the picture back. "I just thank God you changed your mind."

Becky Lee felt an urge to call Maria and thank her for saving her baby.

"So, you have the rest of the day free?" Tad asked.

"Yeah."

"How about we go riding?"

"Horses?"

Tad nodded.

Becky Lee laughed. "I thought you were afraid."

Tad stood and pulled Becky Lee up with him. "It's time I face my fear."

"You don't seem the horse type."

"I can do anything I put my mind to." Tad grabbed her hand and pulled her toward the steps.

"Wait. I want to make a quick phone call first."

Becky Lee went into the kitchen, with Tad behind her, and found the phone book she'd left open on the counter. She located the number and dialed. When someone answered, Becky Lee asked to speak to Maria.

"Who?"

"Maria. She's a technician. I don't know her last name."

"There's no Maria here. Are you sure you have the right number?"

"Yes. I was just there this morning. She did a sonogram for me."

"What's your name?"

"Becky Lee Woodson."

"Hold on a moment, please."

The phone went silent. Becky Lee paced beside the kitchen table. Perhaps Maria had quit already. She hoped she hadn't caused trouble for the nice woman.

"Ms. Woodson?" the voice on the phone said.

"Yes."

"I've checked the staff listing. We don't have any Maria here."

Becky Lee stared at Tad, confused. "I don't understand. She did my sonogram and gave me a picture of my baby. I even heard the heartbeat."

"We don't do that here. And I can't find any record of you being here this morning. I think you called the wrong place. Have a good day." Click.

Becky Lee closed her cell and went back to the phone book. There was only one clinic listed. She compared the number in the phone book to the one she just dialed. They matched.

Tad moved beside her and touched her arm. "Are you okay?"

She shook her head and backed up. "I don't get it." She looked at the phone book once more, then turned to Tad. "Maria was the woman who gave me my picture. But they're saying no one named Maria works there. And that they have no record of me being there."

Tad's face wrinkled in confusion. Then a slow smile worked its way into his eyes. "I know what stopped you from making the wrong choice today. Divine intervention."

Becky Lee narrowed her eyes. "What are you talking about?"

"God provided a different way for you to see your situation. Even in the midst of a place that would have had you doing otherwise. He spoke to you this morning, Bec. And your heart changed."

A peaceful feeling settled over Becky Lee. As odd as it sounded, she believed he was right. Tad's God had spoken to her.

Chapter Twelve

*B*ecky Lee sat in her car in the church parking lot, waiting for Tad, her enlarged belly almost touching the steering wheel. For the past few months, she'd been attending a weekly support group that met at Tad's church on Wednesday nights. The women there had been a big help just by listening. After the first few meetings, she'd opened up and talked about all sorts of things, even Mama and Daddy and Sarah. Sometimes she left crying, other times laughing.

She'd told them about Jesse and how rocky their relationship had been. She confessed that she'd let Jesse leave for Nashville without telling him about the baby. And that even if she wanted to tell him, she didn't know how to find him now. The women expressed concern about her choice, but they seemed to understand. Still, they encouraged her to tell him if he ever showed up in her life again.

Tad had invited her to have dinner with him after this week's meeting. His car sat two empty spaces down from hers, but he wasn't in it. Only two other cars were parked in the lot. She wondered where Tad was and what was keeping him.

Becky Lee rolled down the window, breathed in the warm evening air, and thought about all the changes that had happened in her life over the past five months. Shortly after she graduated from high school, Denise had sold the ranch to Mr. Spencer, boarding Peg and King on a large ranch in the next county.

Denise and Derek got married in June and moved to the city as well. They bought a big house and invited Becky Lee to come live with them, but she wanted to try to make it on her own. So Denise let Becky Lee use some of the money from the sale to move into an apartment in the city and start a new life. She put the rest of the funds into a trust account for when Becky Lee turned twenty-one.

Denise left the travel agency to help Derek with his business. He was still designing the new homes Mr. Spencer wanted built in the old neighborhood, and the heavy paperwork kept her busy full time. The following week, the travel agency hired Becky Lee. She didn't do the same job Denise had done there. Just filed, answered phones, and greeted customers when they came in. But she was learning the business and she found it to be a lot of fun. Especially working with Tad.

Tad had become a close friend. He prayed for her a lot, and Becky Lee figured his prayers were helping, because her life was working out better than she thought it would with Jesse and Denise and the ranch gone, not to mention being pregnant and single.

Tad kept telling her that God cared for her and would provide for her, even though she'd done a lot of stuff she shouldn't have. "All your sins will be forgiven," he'd told her often, "when you accept Jesus as your Savior." She still didn't understand all that stuff, but he kept talking to her about it. Every now and again she asked probing questions. Other times she told him she didn't want to hear it. But it seemed to be sinking in, because she found herself thinking about religious stuff when she was alone, like now.

Becky Lee checked the watch on her swollen wrist. She'd been waiting for twenty minutes. It wasn't like him to be late.

She noticed lights on in the church office. Maybe he was in there. Or perhaps whoever was there would know where Tad was.

After rolling her extra-wide body out of the car, she shuffled to the entry door of the administration building. The reception area was empty. She looked down the hallway. Both sides of the hallway were lined with doors, but all were closed except the one at the very end.

Hearing faint muffled voices, she headed down the hall. As she neared the open door, the words became clear.

"I don't think you understand," said an unfamiliar man's voice.

Not wanting to interrupt a personal conversation, Becky Lee decided to go back and wait in the car. As she turned to leave, she heard her name. She stopped and listened.

"Sure, Becky Lee has made some mistakes." Tad's voice. "But God has been working in her. I can see it. I know you've seen it too."

"You're right, Tad," the other guy said. "I have seen a great change in her. But—"

"If God can forgive her after all she's been through," Tad bellowed, "why can't everyone else?"

"I'm not talking about forgiveness here. You know what the Scripture says about relationships between believers and unbelievers."

"That we are not to be unequally yoked," Tad said quietly. "But if she accepts Christ, everything would be okay."

"You can't force that to happen. It's between her and the Lord."

"I know." His voice sounded strained, defeated.

"God has a great work planned for you. Even if she did come to know the Lord, do you honestly think a new believer could handle being a pastor's wife?"

What? Were they talking about her?

"Are you saying I should put things off?" Tad asked.

"I think you need to choose between pursuing her or pursuing your ministry."

Tad said nothing.

"Only God can answer this question for you. Pray about it. It's obvious that the Lord brought you two together, but it may not be for marriage. Be prepared to accept that. If His purpose for you two is marriage, pray for patience. God will bring you together in His timing if that is His will for you."

I need some air.

Becky Lee hurried back up the hallway as quietly as she could, grateful that the floor was carpeted.

Did Tad really want to marry her?

She rushed through the lobby and out the door. She took several deep breaths of the warm air, then sat on the bench next to the office door.

I shouldn't have gone in there. He can't know I heard all that.

Not wanting him to find her right outside the door, she fled to the car and climbed in.

Why would he want to marry someone with a past like hers? And with a baby on the way? It didn't make sense.

When Tad emerged from the administration building, he went straight to Becky Lee's car. "Sorry I'm late," he said casually through the open window. "Burgers okay?"

"Sure," she said.

"Do you mind if I pick up the food from a drive-through and meet you at your place?" Tad asked, looking as close to stressed out as Becky Lee had ever seen him. "I'm not really in the mood to go out."

"Sounds good to me." She dared not argue.

Tad arrived at her apartment twenty minutes later with a bag of burgers and fries and a cup holder with two drinks.

Becky Lee pushed some magazines off the kitchen table, and they sat there opposite each other. Between bites, she watched Tad. He looked really torn up inside. She wanted to ask him what was going on. But she already knew, and she was afraid to bring up the subject.

"My meeting went real well tonight," she said.

He didn't respond, just put a handful of fries into his mouth and chewed, his gaze focused on the table.

"I think I've got everything just about ready for when the baby comes."

Tad looked up from his food, a confused expression on his face. He shook his head and gave her a half smile. "I'm sorry. I'm being really rude."

"It's all right. I figure even you get stressed sometimes."

"Yeah. Stressed is a good word for it."

"You're always telling me to trust and lean on God, right?"

Tad nodded.

"Doesn't God provide for you when you're in need? I think if he was gonna help anyone, it'd be you."

He laughed. "Yes. He helps me." Tad took in a deep breath and let it out slowly. He played with his paper napkin. "The problem is, sometimes I get too caught up in myself. I ask God for help, but rather than waiting for an answer, I go off and do my own thing. Then I get stressed because I want something that God is saying no to."

Was he referring to marrying her? "So if God said no, would you do whatever you wanted anyway?"

"God has a plan for me. And that plan will come to pass. No matter how bad I might want something else."

Becky Lee swallowed hard. "Can you ever go against God's plans?"

"Yes." Tad fell silent and stared at his hands.

Her heart broke for him. "What will God do if you disobey Him?"

"If I repent, He'll forgive me. But there will probably be natural consequences of my actions. And He won't remove those."

That didn't make sense to Becky Lee. "Why would God forgive, but then allow consequences?

"I'll give you an extreme example to make my point. It's a sin to commit murder, right?

She nodded.

"If a person commits murder and later becomes saved through Christ, his sins are forgiven. But that person will still have to serve time in prison for his crime. That would be the natural consequences for his actions."

Becky Lee looked down at her fat stomach. "Like my baby is the consequence for my bad decisions."

"Bec."

She lifted her head. She saw a sweet sorrow in his eyes.

"Your baby was planned by God. He has a purpose for this little guy…or girl." Tad smiled.

Jenn A. Sesto

Becky Lee was sure he was waiting for her to smile back, but she couldn't. God would never let Tad marry her. Her consequences were spilling over into his life. She was the cause of his struggle.

"Even though your baby was conceived out of wedlock, he or she is still a blessing from God. Yes, things would be different if you'd waited till you were married and a little older, but—"

"But I didn't wait." Guilt overwhelmed her. She hated herself for her past choices. And now, because of her, Tad was hurting too. That wasn't fair. Why would God have let them meet if this was how things were going to be between them? "I'm sorry for getting you in the middle of all this."

Tad's eyes narrowed. "In the middle of what?"

"My messed-up life."

Tad reached across the table and took her hand. "I'm here because I want to be. I promised you I'd be there for you, remember?"

The touch of Tad's hand reminded her of the security she felt with him. He had kept his promise over the past several months. She wished she could feel this secure for the rest of her life. But God didn't want him with her. Tad wanted to marry her, but God was telling him no.

Becky Lee slid her hand back. "You're not supposed to be with me, are you?"

Tad's face twisted in confusion. "What?"

She felt tempted to tell him she'd heard him talking about her earlier. She pushed the thought away. But it arose again. Unable to resist, she blurted, "I heard you at the church tonight. I heard what you and that guy in the office were talking about."

Tad covered his face with his hands. She heard his shallow breaths, then a long sigh. He pulled his hands down and locked into her gaze. He squeezed her hands gently. "I won't deny it. I'm in love you with, Bec."

Her heart pounded. She tried to speak, but her mouth went dry.

"I'm sorry you overheard what you did. It's not the way I had envisioned telling you I want to marry you."

Becky Lee choked on the words she was about to say, but she knew

108

they had to be said. "But you can't marry me. I heard that guy say so." Her voice became shaky. "It's because of everything I've done."

"I don't care what you've done."

"Well, your God does."

A pang of bitterness stirred inside her, accompanied by a sharp pain that shot through her belly. She struggled to breathe.

"Becky Lee, what's wrong?"

His voice sounded far away. She stared at Tad, unable to speak or to understand what he was saying. *Something's wrong.*

She heard Tad talking on the phone. He looked right at her, asked her something…but what?

Two words filtered through her pain-wracked consciousness. "Ambulance. Now."

Chapter Thirteen

ecky Lee looked around the unfamiliar room. Darkness surrounded her, except for a dim light, like a nightlight, by the door. On the far side of the room was a window, the blinds almost shut.

She heard beeping sounds. She looked over her shoulder. Between her and the window were two machines. On one of them, green lines rose and fell on a black screen. The other had numbers on it. Clear bags of liquid hung from a tall metal pole beside her bed. A rubber tube traveled from the bags to her arm: an IV. A blood-pressure cuff tightened around her arm.

Feeling exhausted, Becky Lee closed her eyes. *How did I get here?*

Then she remembered talking with Tad…crying…pain.

My baby!

Her eyes flew open. She touched her stomach. It was far less rounded—almost as flat as before she got pregnant.

My baby's gone.

She tried to lift her head, but it hurt too much.

"Where's my baby?" she screamed.

The door burst open and a nurse rushed in. "Just relax, Becky Lee." She touched her shoulder. "Don't try to sit up just yet." The nurse, a small middle-aged woman, with red hair pulled back in a ponytail, studied the machines. She turned back to Becky Lee, her smile gentle. "I'll have the doctor come in to talk with you. You just lie back and relax."

"Where's my baby?" she asked, her voice raspy and broken.

"You had your baby several of hours ago, honey. A little girl."

"But it's too early." She struggled to sit up.

The nurse touched her shoulder again. "It's important for you to be calm. I'll get the doctor." She hurried out of the room.

"Where's my baby?" Becky Lee called out after her.

How could she leave without telling me anything?

The door opened again. A young man in a white lab coat, who didn't look much older than Tad, came in. While looking at the machines, he said, "Becky Lee, I'm Dr. Swensen. Your doctor is out of town, so I'm covering for him. How are you feeling?"

"Where's my baby?"

Dr. Swensen pulled a chair to the side of the bed and sat in it. "Do you remember coming in here last night?"

"Not really."

"We spoke briefly before taking you into surgery. Do you remember that?"

Becky Lee shook her head.

"That's all right. There was a lot going on when you came in. By the time the ambulance got you here, you were hemorrhaging. Your baby was in severe distress. We had to perform an emergency Cesarean."

"I-Is my baby all right?"

"She's in intensive care."

"What does that mean?"

"Becky Lee, your baby wasn't breathing when she was born."

Becky Lee's own breathing stopped. She imagined her little girl struggling, gasping for air. Her baby could have died. But she was in intensive care now, alive. "Is she gonna be all right?"

"She's suffering from Respiratory Distress Syndrome. She's unable to breathe on her own, so she's on a ventilator. It delivers oxygen and pressure to help keep her lungs inflated. We also gave her an artificial lung surfactant. It's being given to her through a tube that goes into her lungs."

Becky Lee stared at the ceiling, trying to absorb what the doctor was saying. "Is she going to die?"

"That is a possibility. The next couple of days aren't going to be easy for her. But I promise you, we're doing everything we can for her."

Becky Lee closed her eyes. She didn't want to hear any more. This wasn't how things were supposed to turn out. *My baby may die!* A mixture of fear and anger erupted inside her. "Why did this happen?"

The doctor stood and patted Becky Lee's hand. "Why don't you get some sleep. You need your rest."

"I want to know why this happened!"

Dr. Swensen sighed. "Becky Lee, you need to stay calm. For your own health."

He waited for a response, but didn't get one.

He spoke slowly. "You had a placental abruption. By the time the ambulance got you here, the placenta had completely separated from your uterus, which put you and your baby at extreme risk. We almost lost you. But you pulled through the surgery very well. You're a strong young woman."

Strong wasn't the word that came to Becky Lee's mind. Every piece of her being crumbled. She was trapped in a living nightmare. "What happens now?"

"You'll stay here in ICU for at least twenty-four hours for monitoring." The doctor glanced over his shoulder at the machines, then looked back at her. "Do you have any other questions?"

"No." She just wanted to be alone.

"The young man who called the ambulance for you is in the waiting room. Is there anything you'd like me to tell him?"

Tad was there? A shimmer of hope rose in her, but it quickly diminished as the memory of their last conversation crashed into her head. The bitterness she'd felt last night resurfaced. She held her breath, trying to keep herself from exploding. "No," she said quietly,

"Your sister is here too. I can allow her to come in since she's family."

Through clenched teeth, she replied, "I just want to be alone for a while."

Dr. Swensen gave a small smile. "I understand. Get some rest. Maybe later today, you'll be able to get up and see your baby. You won't be able to hold—"

"I don't want to see my baby," she lashed out. "Not with tubes sticking in her. Now, leave me alone."

The doctor's face tensed. "Okay. I'll be back to check on you." He left the room, closing the door behind him.

Becky Lee wanted to scream. Stomp her feet and throw something. Grab that doctor and shake him until he took back everything he'd just said.

But none of that would change the truth.

Chapter Fourteen

Becky Lee lay in her hospital bed, staring at the ceiling. How had her life turned so upside down? A tear slipped down the side of her face onto the thin white pillow.

Denise poked her head around the privacy curtain. "Good, you're awake." She crossed to the window and pulled open the blinds. The bright sunshine stung Becky Lee's eyes.

"The ICE nurses let me see your baby through the ICU window again. She is so cute. You really should see her." A touch of sadness damped her cheery voice.

"No, thanks." In the five days since her baby was born, Becky Lee hadn't seen her child once. She couldn't risk getting attached, not yet.

Denise plopped into the visitor's chair at the foot of Becky Lee's bed. "The doctor says you're doing fine. You should be able to go home tomorrow."

"Good," Becky Lee said in a flat tone. "Then you can go back home too."

Denise stood. "No way. I told Derek I'm staying at your apartment until that precious baby of yours is safe at home with her mommy."

Becky Lee couldn't bring herself to share in her sister's glee.

"Then we can talk more about you and that darling little girl coming to our place." Denise crossed to her sister's bedside, her face aglow. "There's plenty of room, and you can stay as long as you need to."

"I don't know," Becky Lee mumbled. "I really don't know about anything right now."

Dr. Swensen came into the room, chart in hand. "Good morning," he said cheerfully.

Becky Lee did not return his smile.

"I have good news. Your newborn's condition has stabilized."

"What's that mean?"

"It means she's not getting worse," Denise said. "Right, Doctor?"

He nodded. "She'll have to stay in the hospital for another week or so. But the prognosis is encouraging."

Becky Lee lifted her head. "Are the tubes gone?"

"Well, no." Dr. Swensen looked at Denise, then back at Becky Lee. "She's still on the respirator, and she will need the feeding tube for a little while longer."

She lay back down on the pillow. "I don't wanna see her till all the tubes are out."

Denise took Becky Lee's hand in hers. "Honey, she's premature. Her healing will take a while."

Becky Lee pulled her hand away. Obviously, her sister had no idea what she was going through.

Dr. Swensen stepped closer. "She needs to know her mama loves her. It may help her progress if you go talk to her, touch her."

"I can't. Not with all that stuff on her."

Denise's eyes misted. "Honey, you'll be going home tomorrow. Why don't you spend some time with her while you're here. It'll be difficult, I know, but it's important, for you and for her."

Becky Lee closed her eyes. She didn't want to see her baby. She couldn't let herself get close to this child who might not make it through the week.

But I do want to see her! She wanted to count her daughter's little fingers and tiny toes. Wanted to look into her face and see if she recognized any of her own features. Or Denise's. Maybe even a hint of something from their parents.

Then she thought about seeing her child hooked up to all kinds of tubes and monitors. She couldn't face that. Besides, if the little girl didn't survive, which seemed likely, the grief wouldn't be so bad if she'd never seen the kid in the first place. No. She would not go see that baby. No matter how hard everyone tried to make her do it.

But I want to hold my daughter. Tears formed on Becky Lee's lashes. It seemed no matter what she chose to do, she'd be making the wrong decision.

"Okay," she said softly. "I'll go see her."

❦ ❦ ❦

The short walk down the hall to the ICU nursery felt like a ten-mile hike. Dr. Swensen held Becky Lee's arm on one side, Denise on the other. Every step made her hurt all over.

As they passed the regular nursery, Becky Lee tried to turn away. She did not want to see all those healthy babies, especially not right before seeing her own preemie for the first time. But her pace was too slow to just zip past. Finally, she gave in and peeked through the window.

Behind the glass, she saw about ten transparent cribs with newborns, some squirming, others fast asleep. They all looked perfect and beautiful. "They're so tiny."

"Yes," Dr. Swensen said. "And remember, your baby is even smaller. She's only four and a half pounds right now. Most of these babies are seven pounds or more."

"It's amazing how two or three pounds can make such a difference," Denise said.

At the end of the glass wall, they turned a corner, and Dr. Swensen led Becky Lee through some double doors. Three nurses sat behind a long counter. One was on the phone, another sat at a computer, and the third stood studying a file. Behind the nurse's station was a wall with a window, similar to the nursery but smaller.

I can't do this.

The slow-moving threesome stopped at the desk. The nurse with the file looked up. Her face softened into a sweet smile.

"You must be Becky Lee," she said. "I'm Lorraine. I've been taking care of your sweet little girl. I know she'd love to see her mama. Would you like to come with me?"

Becky Lee looked at Dr. Swensen. He nodded. She looked at Denise. Tears glistened in her eyes. Becky Lee took a deep breath to keep from crying.

"You can do this, honey," Denise assured her. She and Dr. Swensen released her into the nurse's care.

Lorraine led Becky Lee through another set of double doors that had the word *Restricted* on them in bright red letters. She took her to a small bathroom to wash her hands. "You won't be able to hold your baby because of all the tubes. But you can touch her and talk to her and stroke her skin. She'll like that."

Lorraine opened the door to the nursery, and Becky Lee followed her in. Four tiny babies lay in bassinettes, each hooked up with tubes and wires to some kind of machine. They all looked so helpless. Becky Lee choked up so badly, she could hardly breathe.

Lorraine stopped at the second baby bed from the door. "Here's your beautiful little girl."

Becky Lee gasped at the tiny body. Wires poked into the skinny arms and legs, and a thin tube taped to her mouth went down her throat. Her arms and legs moved as if she wanted to get away from this place.

Then the premature infant opened her eyes. She looked up at her mother, and her thrashing stilled. Becky Lee felt as if everything disappeared except for her and her baby. Time seemed to stop.

"You can touch her," Lorraine reminded her.

Becky Lee reached into the little bed to touch her leg, but pulled back.

"Go ahead," Lorraine said. "Talk to her."

"I-I don't know what to say," Becky Lee choked out.

"Whatever comes to your mind."

She reached out again, this time touching her daughter's soft skin. The tiny leg moved. "Hi, Baby Girl. I …I'm your mama."

The little eyes crinkled and seemed to light up at the sound of her voice.

Becky Lee looked up and saw Denise gazing through the window. She smiled. Through streams of tears, she said, "My baby girl."

Her sister nodded and smiled back.

❦ ❦ ❦

Becky Lee sat up in her hospital bed, resting alone. All she could think about was her little girl. She'd been excited to finally see her. But images of the tiny, helpless body strapped to monitors assaulted her.

She heard a knock, and the door opened. Tad came in, a sly grin on his face. He zipped open his jacket and pulled out a paper bag and cup from the local fast-food burger joint.

"Double cheeseburger, large fries, and a strawberry milkshake, as promised." He glanced over his shoulder as he arranged the items on the bedside tray. "You'll have to eat this in a hurry, before the nurse finds out. I was sure the smell would give me away before I got here."

Becky Lee cracked a smile, but she didn't look at him. She'd been looking forward to seeing him when she talked to him on the phone earlier, but now she just wanted to be alone.

Tad rolled the food tray over to her lap.

"Would you mind just leaving it? I'm not really hungry after all. Maybe I'll eat some a little later."

Tad pulled a chair to the side of the bed and sat in it. "I talked to Denise. She said you saw your baby."

Becky Lee nodded. Why couldn't he just leave her alone?

"She's a cutie, isn't she?"

Tears formed.

"The nurses say she's getting better every day."

"Please stop," Becky Lee said around the lump in her throat. "I don't want to talk about it right now."

"It's hard, I know."

"No, you don't know," she lashed out. "You have no idea what I'm going through."

Tad pulled in a deep breath. "You're right. I don't. I'm sorry."

"Why would God do this to a little baby? That baby never did anything to anybody! But she's struggling to stay alive. She shouldn't be suffering for my mistake."

"Becky." Tad closed his eyes for a moment, then opened them again. "I know it's hard to accept things like this. We don't always understand the reasons things happen. But God *is* in control."

"Really? Then why did He let me get pregnant if He was just gonna take my baby away from me?"

"Sometimes situations like this draw us closer to Him. He wants us to lean on Him and rely on Him to help us get through. Trust Him, Bec. He'll take care of you and your baby."

"Like he took care of my parents?" Becky Lee snapped. "And my best friend?"

"Bec—"

"And now this God you want me to believe in is gonna take my baby girl."

"Don't say that," Tad said, his voice choking. "Your daughter's going to be fine."

"Why? Because God loves me? No. He doesn't care about me. He's just keeping her alive for a while to make me suffer for my sins. Then He's gonna take her. And why shouldn't He? I deserve the consequences."

"Becky Lee, please don't do this to yourself. "

"I want you to leave now, Tad. Right now."

Tears clouded Tad's eyes, but he didn't say another word. He just nodded and left.

As soon as the door shut behind him, Becky Lee burst out crying. She pushed the food tray away and lay back on the pillow. She closed her eyes and wept until sleep overtook her.

"Mama, Mama, come here! Hurry, Mama."

I run out the back door, thinking she's hurt. But when I get outside I see my sweet little Julianna riding her bike without training wheels.

"Look, Mama, I can do it. See?"

"Yes, Sweetie, I see. You're doing it all on your own."

"Daddy helped me. He showed me how."

Curiosity makes me turn around. Sunshine blinds my eyes. But I see someone walking toward me. A man. He's smiling, but I can't make out his face. As he gets closer, my eyes adjust. It's—

"Becky Lee, wake up."

She opened her eyes and saw Denise standing next to her.

"Honey, it's almost time to go home. The doctor will be in soon to do a final check. Then you'll fill out some paperwork and that's it. You're out of here."

Becky Lee barely understood her sister's words. She wanted to get back to the dream, find out who the man was she was about to see.

"I've got a wonderful dinner planned. You'll be able to go home and just relax."

"I want to see my baby before I leave."

"Of course. We'll take whatever time you need. And we'll come back every day until she's ready to come home."

"Home? To my apartment or your house?"

"That's up to you. You know I'd love for you to come back with me."

"That probably would be best."

Denise's eyes shone. "Great. We'll start making plans tonight." She squeezed her sister's hand. "I'll go see what's keeping the doctor."

Becky Lee lay back in the bed. She tried to recapture the details of the dream. Her baby wasn't a baby anymore. She was maybe four or five, just learning how to ride a bike. Her name was Julianna. She called someone daddy.

Jenn A. Sesto

Did the dream foretell the future? Would her baby get better and grow up to be a normal, healthy child? With a daddy around? If so, who would it be?

Chapter Fifteen

Becky Lee felt much better being home at her apartment. No nurses coming in and out of the room, checking on her all the time. No beeping machines. All was quiet except the sounds of Denise cooking in the kitchen.

There was just one problem. Becky Lee's baby girl was still at the hospital. It didn't seem right not having her home.

The aromas of garlic bread and pasta sauce wafted into the living room, where Becky Lee sat in her daddy's recliner. She grew hungrier each time she inhaled.

She felt truly grateful for her sister's presence. Not just to cook, but just being there.

"Dinner's ready." Denise carried in two plates piled high with spaghetti and garlic bread. She handed one to Becky Lee and set hers on the end table between the recliner and sofa. "Want to listen to some music while we eat?" she asked.

Becky Lee shrugged.

Denise turned on the stereo and popped in a CD. Christian music poured out of the speakers.

The lyrics bothered Becky Lee a little. But she figured her sister could listen to whatever she wanted after all she'd been doing for her.

Between bites, Denise said, "I'm sorry you're having to go through all this. I wish there was more I could do for you."

"You're doing plenty. I'm sure Derek isn't very happy about you being away."

"He wants me to stay as long as you need me." She paused. "He's still okay with you coming to live with us."

"I can't think about that right now."

"There's no rush. We'll take one day at a time, okay?" Denise took a bite of her spaghetti. "So, have you decided on a name yet?"

Becky Lee thought about her dream. "I was thinking about Julianna."

"I love it. Where did you come up with that?"

"It came to me last night. I don't know for sure, though." She wondered whether she should even name her baby. "Denise...what if she dies?"

Her sister reached over from the sofa and squeezed Becky Lee's hand. "I wish I could tell you that won't happen. But I can tell you that God's hand is in this. We're all praying for her: Tad, Derek, everyone at church."

"Do you really believe God will save her?"

"I don't know. His purposes don't always make sense to us. I mean, I don't understand why Mama and Daddy had to die. But I think their deaths brought you and me closer to Him."

"What are you talking about?"

"Mama and Daddy didn't teach us about Jesus. If they hadn't died, Derek and I would have just gotten married and moved away. But we waited. I stayed at the ranch and got that job at the travel agency. That's where I met Tad. Then I took you to that party, where you met him."

Becky Lee twirled her fork in the pile of pasta. She thought about how her life had changed since meeting Tad. "He wants to marry me."

Denise's eyebrows raised in surprise. "He proposed?"

"No. But the night my baby was born I overheard him talking to someone in the church office. I think it was the pastor. He talked about wanting to marry me, but the pastor tried to talk him out of it."

"Why?"

"Something about there being too much pressure and the timing not being right. He told Tad to pray about it." Becky Lee dipped her bread in the sauce and took a bite.

"But he hasn't said anything to you?"

"We started to talk about it, but then…the baby came. Yesterday was the first time we've talked since she was born. But I kinda blew up on him and kicked him out."

"He told me about that."

"When?"

"He came by last night while you were sleeping."

"I'm surprised he came back after I attacked him and his God."

"God isn't just Tad's God. He's for everyone. He doesn't force anyone to follow Him, but He does speak to all of us."

"He doesn't speak to me."

"Yes, he does."

"You didn't get an abortion, did you?"

Becky Lee remembered that day at the clinic when Maria had saved her baby. But after the fact, no one knew who Maria was.

"And do you think meeting Tad was an accident? God put you two on the same path. He has His hands on your life, whether you realize it or not."

God had His hands on her life, all right. And He wasn't going to let anything happen between her and Tad. She wanted to voice that argument to Denise, but she didn't have the energy to get into it. "I'm really tired. And I want to get up early in the morning to go to the hospital. Do you mind if I go to bed now?"

"Not at all." Denise stood and reached for Becky Lee's plate.

Once she managed to get out of the recliner, Becky Lee turned to Denise. "Thanks for being here."

Her sister set the plate on the coffee table and hugged her tight. "I love you."

Becky Lee had rarely heard her sister say those words. Though she loved Denise, too, she wasn't able to say it back.

As Becky Lee walked toward her bedroom, Denise turned down the volume on the music.

Becky Lee stopped at the hall doorway. "Please leave it on. I'm starting to like it."

❧ ❧ ❧

Over the clanking of the dishes, Becky Lee could still hear Denise's music. The volume wasn't real loud, but she heard something about Jesus telling people to come to Him and He would give them rest. She wondered if He'd really said that. And if He had, who He was talking to.

Had God really been speaking to her, like Denise said? Was He really in control of what was happening in her life, in her baby's life? But if God were in control, why would He put that little girl through all this stuff?

Did God talk to people in dreams too? Like the one she'd had about the daddy helping her daughter ride a bike? Did that mean she was going to make it and have a father? Or was that just her wishful thinking working overtime?

It was just a dream, she scoffed. *It doesn't mean anything.*

The song ended and another began. Becky Lee listened closely to the words. The lyrics spoke about someone who was stressed out, who had a lot of trials going on. The person couldn't take it anymore, but didn't know what to do.

The fast-tempo music stopped abruptly, then the artist sang softly, "Be still, and know that I am God." The music picked up again.

Strangely, Becky Lee's heart felt peaceful and comforted. She drifted off to sleep.

❧ ❧ ❧

Nothing seems familiar anymore, except for one or two of the houses along the road. It seems like I've been driving forever.

"Are we there yet, Mama?" asks a small voice from the backseat.

I look over my shoulder and see a little boy in a car seat, holding a toy truck. He's about three years old.

"Yeah, Mom, how much longer?" Julianna sits next to me in the passenger seat. She's about eight.

"Just a little farther," I reply.

Suddenly we aren't in the car anymore. The three of us are walking down a path, with thick brush all around us. After a little while, we come to a clearing with a big swimming hole. There's a blanket and picnic basket on the sand. And a man sitting on a large rock. He looks like he's praying.

"Daddy!" Both of the kids run toward the man. He turns at the sound of their voices. I strain my eyes to see his face.

He bends over to hug the kids. He picks up the little boy and takes Julianna's hand, then walks toward me. I still can't see his face.

"I thought you'd never get here," he says.

I recognize that voice. It's Tad!

❦ ❦ ❦

Becky Lee woke up with a jolt. Sun streamed in through the almost-closed blinds. She heard Denise in the kitchen and smelled bacon cooking. She looked at the clock on the nightstand: eight thirty. She grabbed her robe and went to the kitchen.

"How'd you sleep?" Denise asked.

"Like a rock. I don't think I moved all night."

"Good. You needed that. Breakfast should be ready in a few minutes. Then we can head over to the hospital."

"Sounds good."

"Do you mind if I drop you off and come back later to get you?"

"No. Where you going?"

"It's Sunday. I'd like to go to church. I'll come back as soon as the service is over."

"What time does it start?"

"Ten."

"Could I come with you?"

Denise stopped cracking eggs and turned to stare at her sister. "You want to come?"

"Yeah. If we hurry, we can stop at the hospital to see Julianna, then go to church. I can go back again afterward."

"Of course we can do that." Denise hugged her sister. "I'm so glad you want to go."

❧ ❧ ❧

At the hospital, the nurse Lorraine told Becky Lee that Julianna's condition hadn't changed. That was good news, but Becky Lee still found it difficult to look at her daughter with all those tubes in her.

Becky Lee told Lorraine she'd be gone for an hour or so, but that she could call her cell phone if anything changed.

She and Denise walked into the church a few minutes late. The pastor was already on stage, engaged in his sermon. The pews were full, but the girls found seats in the back. Becky Lee was glad about that. She would've been embarrassed walking down that long aisle, feeling as if everyone were looking at her and judging her for being tardy.

After she settled in her seat, Becky Lee focused on the words that were being spoken. The pastor was talking about a guy named David and what a great warrior he was.

"Romans 3:23 says, 'For all have sinned and fall short of the glory of God.' Even King David fell short. But God called David 'a man after My own heart.' How could God say that after what David did?"

Who was this King David and what had he done?

"Read with me beginning in Second Samuel, chapter 11, verse 2."

Denise pulled out the Bible from the rack in the pew in front of them. She flipped through the pages till she found the verse the pastor was referring to and used her finger to follow along. She scooted closer to Becky Lee. Becky Lee leaned in and read as the pastor continued.

"Then it happened one evening that David arose from his bed and walked on the roof of the king's house. And from the roof he saw a woman bathing, and the woman was very beautiful to behold."

The pastor crossed the stage, speaking out to the audience. "David was curious about this woman, so he asked about her. He found out that Bathsheba was the wife of Uriah, one of his soldiers. So what does David do?" The pastor looked back at the Bible on the podium. "Verse 4 says, 'Then David sent messengers, and took her; and she came to him, and he lay with her.' Then verse 5: 'And the woman conceived; so she sent and told David, and said, 'I am with child.'"

This man of God had an affair with a married woman and got her pregnant? And his story was in the Bible?

"David broke two commandments here. 'Thou shalt not covet thy neighbor's wife' and 'Thou shalt not commit adultery.' This man, who sought God for everything and trusted Him with all his heart, fell short."

Fell short? He majorly screwed up.

"When David found out Bathsheba was pregnant, he plotted to kill Uriah. Verse 14 says, 'In the morning it happened that David wrote a letter to Joab and sent it by hand of Uriah. And he wrote a letter, saying, "Set Uriah in the forefront of the hottest battle, and retreat from him, that he may be struck down and die."' He even sent this letter by the hands of the man he intended to have killed. How could David do such a thing? How could *anyone* do such a thing?"

He tried to get the woman's husband killed? And I thought what I did was bad. Becky Lee shook her head in disbelief.

"In chapter 12, verse 9, God says to David, 'Why have you despised the commandment of the Lord, to do evil in His sight? You have killed Uriah, the Hittite, with the sword; you have taken his wife to be your wife.'"

A murderer in the Bible! Imagine that.

"In verse 13, David admits, 'I have sinned against the Lord.' Then Nathan the prophet told David, 'The Lord also has put away your sin; you shall not die. However, because by this deed…the child also who is born to you shall surely die.' Scripture then tells us, 'And the Lord struck the child that Uriah's wife bore to David, and it became ill. Then on the seventh day it came to pass that the child died.'"

Becky Lee gasped. God killed the baby. That was David's punishment. Would God do the same with Julianna?

"Several of the psalms tell of David's repenting and confessing his guilt. I'd like to read to you a few verses from Psalm 51. 'Have mercy upon me, O God, according to Your loving kindness; according to the multitude of Your tender mercies, blot out my transgressions. Wash me thoroughly from my iniquity, and cleanse me from my sin. For I acknowledge my transgressions, and my sin is always before me. Against You, You only, have I sinned, and done this evil in Your sight, that You may be found just when You speak and blameless when You judge.'"

David repented and confessed his sins. But that wouldn't bring his baby back. How could David not be angry with God?

"David had consequences to pay for his actions, but God still forgave him of his sins. Murder. Adultery. Covetousness. God will forgive you too. Do you carry guilt for sins you've committed? Why haven't you asked God for forgiveness and let Him free you? Is it because you believe your sins are so bad that you cannot possibly be forgiven?"

Yes. That's exactly how she felt.

"The good news is, you're wrong. God is not a god of guilt. Satan wants you to feel guilty. But through Jesus Christ, our Savior, we are forgiven and freed. We are handed the gift of eternal life."

Freed from guilt? Was that possible? She listened for more.

"Ephesians 2, verses 8 and 9, says, 'For by grace you have been saved through faith, and that not of yourselves; it is the gift of God, not of works, lest anyone should boast.' We don't have to do good works or give burnt offerings. By our faith and God's grace we are saved. No matter what you've done, you will be forgiven. All you have to do is ask. Pray right now, just where you are. Ask God to forgive you in the name of His Son, Jesus Christ."

Becky Lee felt as if the pastor were talking directly to her. Tears burned in her eyes and a heavy feeling tightened her chest. She wanted to be forgiven…to be rid of the horrible feelings about what she'd done. She longed to be set free of the guilt she felt. But she didn't know what to say or how to pray.

The pastor descended the steps of the stage and opened his arms. "Is there anyone here today who hasn't given his or her life to the Lord? Anyone who's not sure you're going to heaven? Do you want to be forgiven? Set free from your sins? Have the promise of eternal life? If so, please come forward. There's someone here who will pray with you. The Bible says, 'If you confess with your mouth, "Jesus is Lord," and believe in your heart that God has raised Him from the dead, you will be saved.'"

Everyone in the church stood and started singing. Three people walked up to the front and knelt on the steps. Then two more.

Becky Lee saw Tad up there, kneeling with a young girl, possibly a year or two younger than herself.

Her thoughts went back to Julianna. What would happen if her baby died? Would she go to heaven? Would God take care of her? If she lived, would He take care of her?

In her head, Becky Lee heard a gentle, loving voice urge, "Let go. Let go."

She stood and started walking toward the stage, her feet moving almost without her mind telling them to. All the way down the aisle, she felt as if she were leaning on someone.

As she came up to the steps, a lady with a pretty smile held out her hand, as if she knew it would be difficult for Becky Lee to kneel because of the surgery. They knelt together.

"What's your name?" the woman asked softly.

"Becky Lee."

"Becky Lee, are you ready to commit your life to Jesus Christ?"

She nodded.

"Can we pray right here?"

"I-I don't know how to pray. I wouldn't know what to say."

"Just tell the Lord whatever's in your heart right now."

"Okay." She bowed her head. "Dear God . . ." She looked up at the woman.

The woman smiled. "It's all right. Go on."

Becky Lee closed her eyes. "God, I ...I have sinned. A lot. And because of my sins, my baby might die. If she does, I'll accept it as my consequence. I give my little girl to you, God, because I can't help her..." She couldn't get out any more words. She couldn't stop crying.

The lady put her arm around her and hugged her tightly.

Becky Lee tried again. "I believe Jesus died for me so I can be forgiven. I am giving up control of my life to You, Jesus. I'm letting go. I surrender."

She had never felt so free in all her life.

Chapter Sixteen

The minute Becky Lee stepped out of the church, Denise grabbed her and gave her a big hug. "Praise the Lord," she whispered, her voice cracking.

Becky Lee pulled away and looked at her sister, tears streaming down her cheeks.

"What's wrong?" Denise asked.

"Nothing," she answered quietly. A heavy weight had lifted from her while she was inside the church, but another one pressed down so fiercely she had trouble breathing. The anxiety was so repulsive, she thought she would be sick. All she could think about was Julianna and whether she would be alive when she saw her again. "Can we go back to the hospital now?"

"Of course. I told Tad he could come with us. Do you mind?"

"No." More people filed out of the church and gathered outside the entrance. Some stopped to talk to those who had accepted Jesus that morning. Becky Lee wanted to escape before anyone stopped to talk to her. She did not want to delay getting to the hospital any more than she already had.

"Can I have the keys?" Becky Lee asked. "I'd like to wait in the car while you find Tad."

"No problem." She tossed her the car keys. "Are you okay?"

"Yeah. I just need to see my baby once more time before…" She couldn't bring herself to say it. But she knew in her heart that God was going to take her baby. Soon.

❦ ❦ ❦

The drive to the hospital was quiet. Becky Lee leaned against the headrest, her eyes closed. She didn't want to look at anyone, afraid she'd start crying again.

She'd thought she would be happier when she accepted Christ as her Savior. But a deep sadness tore at her heart. Still, at the same time she felt a strange peace.

God, she prayed, *I give Julianna to You. You can take her if that's your will. Just please let me see her one more time.*

When they arrived at the hospital, they took the elevator up to the fourth floor. Lorraine sat at the nurse's station, studying a chart. She looked up as soon as she heard Becky Lee come up.

"I've been trying to reach you, but I kept getting your voice mail," she said quickly.

Becky Lee's heart stopped. *We're too late. She's dead.*

As Lorraine came around the counter, Tad put an arm around Becky Lee and gave her a reassuring squeeze.

"Come look," Lorraine said.

Denise held on to Becky Lee's other arm. The three of them followed the nurse to the window. Julianna's crib was empty.

Becky Lee's knees went limp. She only remained standing because Tad and Denise held her up.

Lorraine pointed to a corner of the room. A nurse sat in a rocking chair, holding a baby, feeding her with a bottle.

Not just a baby. My baby!

Becky Lee touched the window. "She…she's off the…."

Lorraine smiled, her eyes glistening. "Let's go feed your baby girl."

Epilogue

ecky Lee put the last glass in the dishwasher, then glanced around her kitchen. All she had left to do was wipe the counters down after preparing all the snacks. In about a half hour, ten little girls would be arriving to celebrate Julianna's sixth birthday. She'd personally picked out all the games she and her friends were going to play. She had even helped bake the cake and put together the party bags, filling them with candy and little toys.

"Mama, look what I got!" Julianna ran into the kitchen with a purple satin dress in her hands.

Becky Lee wiped her hands on a towel and bent down to see the new dress. "That's very pretty." Even though Becky Lee already knew, she asked, "Who gave it to you?"

"It was a present from Daddy. He wants me to wear it today." Julianna jumped up and down. "Can I, Mama, please?"

"Of course, sweetie. Where is your daddy?"

"He went to the barn to feed Peg and King." A sheepish grin played on Julianna's face. "He forgot to feed them earlier this morning. But he didn't want me to tell you."

Becky Lee couldn't help but chuckle. "Well your daddy has been very busy setting up for your party. Did he get the piñata up?"

Her face lit up. "Yeah. It's in the tree out front. You should come see it."

"I will. I just need to finish up in here, then get changed." She pulled on the hem of her shirt. "Someone splattered cake batter all over me."

Julianna's cheeks reddened. "I didn't mean to."

"I know. Come here." Becky Lee hugged her precious daughter and kissed her on the top of her curly head. "Now, go get changed. Your friends are going to be here soon."

Julianna raced out of the kitchen and skipped up the stairs.

Becky Lee closed the dishwasher and washed down the counters. She then went upstairs to her room. Country music played from the clock radio on her nightstand. She must have forgotten to turn it off this morning. Letting it play, she grabbed a clean T-shirt out of her clothes drawer and quickly changed.

She crossed the room and glanced out the window. Tad wasn't in sight, but the two horses stood in the corral, eating hay from their feed bins. She'd been thrilled on the day Tad told her she could buy them back from the ranch they'd been boarded at since Denise sold their parents' place. She had feared she wouldn't be able to afford to keep them and might eventually have to sell them. But God didn't let that happen.

Her gaze shifted to the structure that would soon be a fully enclosed four-stall barn. It was close to being done; they just needed to get the roof on before winter. But that was a couple of months away, so she wasn't worried. She felt thankful that Tad's family had deeded the land to them as a wedding gift. The contractor had finished building their house last month, shortly after their first anniversary.

"Bec?"

She turned toward the hallway as he entered the room.

"Are you ready?"

"Yes. Did you set up the table and chairs out front?"

Tad swept Becky Lee into his arms. "Yes, ma'am." He grinned, then kissed her softly on the lips. He pulled back, his eyes twinkling. "We have about a half hour, right?"

She smiled and shot him a suspicious look. "Why?"

"Because I want you to go into the bathroom and take that test you've been putting off for the last two days."

"Now?"

Tad took Becky Lee's hand and pulled her toward the closed bathroom door. "I'll wait for you out here."

"But—"

The song on the radio ended and the DJ's words blared out of the small black box on the nightstand. "And now here's the song I promised. It's by a new artist, fresh out of Nashville. Here's Jesse McCoy with *I've Been Searching for You.*"

So Jesse had made it big after all.

Tad hurried over and turned off the radio. He looked back at Becky Lee, his eyes clouded. Her heart filled with dread at the realization that a part of her past was rearing its ugly head.

Becky Lee had talked with Tad several times over the last six years about what she would do if she located Jesse or if he came back around. They agreed she'd have to tell him about Julianna. Jesse would surely want to know who she was.

When Julianna was a couple of months old, Becky Lee had attempted to find the agent Jesse went to see before graduation. But Jesse had already moved on to a different agent. So she'd let the idea go, figuring she would deal with it if the opportunity ever presented itself.

Tad pulled her close. "Don't worry about this. Not today."

Her voice cracked. "I guess I knew someday I'd have to face him."

Tad caressed her hair. "We'll get through this together."

Becky Lee sank into Tad's shoulder. She knew he was right. Everything would work out somehow.

"Will you go take that test now?" Tad asked, renewed excitement in his voice.

Her heart immediately lifted. "Yes. I will."

The doorbell rang.

Tad pointed to the bathroom door. "I'll answer it. You get in there."

Jenn A. Sesto

After he left, Becky Lee shut the door behind her. As she looked at her reflection in the mirror, she thought about Jesse. She wondered if he'd want to be a part of Julianna's life. She wondered if he'd hate her for not telling him about his child. But back then, she was so sure that not telling him was the right thing to do.

With shaky hands, Becky Lee opened the medicine cabinet and took the pregnancy test kit off the shelf. She took off the plastic wrap and opened the box. After pulling out the contents, she read the instructions. They were simple enough to follow.

Moments later, she sat on the edge of the tub with the white stick beside her. She focused on her watch, not wanting to look too soon. Her eagerness rose with each movement of the second hand around the face.

Julianna burst into the bedroom. "Mama, Aunt Denise is here."

"I'll be out in a minute. You go on downstairs."

"Okay!"

She glanced at the closed bathroom door. As her gaze returned to her watch, a dark blue color at the tip of the white stick caught her eye. She picked it up. "Oh, my gosh!" A scream came out of her mouth. "I'm pregnant!"

She opened the door just as Denise and Julianna came running into the room.

"Are you all right?" her sister asked.

"I'm so glad you're here." She ran up to Denise and gave her a hug.

"Mama?"

She bent down to Julianna. "I'm okay, honey." She stroked her little girl's blonde curls.

Tad hustled into the room past Denise. The light shining in his eyes told her he'd figured it out. He whisked her off her feet and spun her around. Their laughter filled the room.

Denise picked up Julianna. "Hey, are you guys going to let us in on your secret?"

Tad set Becky Lee down.

"We're pregnant," she exclaimed.

Denise's eyes grew big. "Really? That's great." She gave Becky Lee a one-handed hug and danced around with Julianna in her arms. "Did you hear that, sweetie? You're going to have a baby brother or sister."

Julianna laughed. Tad pulled his wife into his arms and held her tight. "A baby," he whispered.

Thank You, Lord, Becky Lee prayed. *In spite of all I've done wrong, and haven't done right, You have given me far more than I ever could have imagined. Thank You, Lord!*